NORA ROBERTS

A WORLD APART
&
THE WITCHING HOUR

piatkus

PIATKUS

This edition first published in Great Britain in 2013 by Piatkus
Reprinted 2013 (twice)

Copyright © Nora Roberts 2013

Previously published separately:
A World Apart originally published in the US by Penguin Putnam Inc.
in the collection Once Upon a Kiss in 2002
First published separately in Great Britain in eBook format in 2012
by Hachette Digital
Copyright © Nora Roberts 2002
The Witching Hour originally published in the US by Penguin Putnam Inc.
in the collection Once Upon a Midnight in 2003
First published separately in Great Britain in eBook format in 2012
by Hachette Digital
Copyright © Nora Roberts 2003

The moral right of the author has been asserted.

*All characters and events in this publication, other than those
clearly in the public domain, are fictitious and any resemblance
to real persons, living or dead, is purely coincidental.*

A CIP catalogue record for this book is available from the British Library.

ISBN 978-0-7499-5877-0

Typeset in Bembo by M Rules
Printed and bound by CPI Group (UK) Ltd, Croydon, CR0 4YY

Papers used by Piatkus are from well-managed forests
and other responsible sources.

MIX
Paper from
responsible sources
FSC® C104740

Piatkus
An imprint of
Little, Brown Book Group
100 Victoria Embankment
London EC4Y 0DY

An Hachette UK Company
www.hachette.co.uk

www.piatkus.co.uk

A WORLD APART

1

In the sweltering jungle, under the blood-red sun, Kadra hunted. Her steps were silent, her eyes – green as the trio of stones that encrusted the hilt of her sword – were alert, watchful, merciless.

For four days and four nights she had tracked her prey, over the Stone Mountains, beyond the Singing River, and into the verdant heat of the Land of Tulle.

What she stalked rarely ventured to these borders, and she herself had never traveled so far in the south of A'Dair.

There were villages here, small enclaves of lesser hunters, settlements of farmers and weavers with their young and their animals. The young were as much food to what she hunted as the cattle and mounts were.

She trod on the mad red flowers that were strewn on the path, ignored the sly silver slide of a snake down the trunk of a tree. She saw, sensed, scented both, but they were of no interest to her.

The Bok demons were her only interest now, and destroying them her only goal.

It was what she had been born for.

Other scents came to her – the beasts, large and small, that inhabited the jungle, and the thick, wet fragrance of vine and blossom. The blood – no longer fresh – of one that had been caught and consumed by what she hunted.

She passed a great fall of water that raged over the cliffs to pound its drumbeat into the river below. Though she had never walked upon this ground, this she knew by its light and music as a sacred place. One that no demon could enter. So she stopped to drink of its purifying waters, to fill her water bag for the journey yet to come.

And poured drops from her hand to the ground in thanks to the powers of life.

Beyond the falls, the busier scents of people – sweat, flesh, cooking, springwater from a village well – reached her keen senses.

It was her duty to protect them, and her fate that none among them could ever be her companion, her friend, her lifemate. These were truths she had never questioned.

At last she caught the overripe stench that was Bok.

The sword streaked out of its sheath, a bright battle sound as she pivoted on the heels of her soft leather boots. The dagger, its point a diamond in the sun, flipped from its wrist mount to her hand.

The dark blue claws of the Bok that had leaped from a branch overhead whizzed past her face, missing their mark. She set into a fighting stance and waited for his next charge.

It looked oddly normal. Other than those lethal retractable claws, the scent, the needle-sharp fangs that snapped out when the lips were peeled back for battle, the Bok looked no different from the people they devoured at every opportunity.

This one was small for his species, no more than six feet, which put him on a level with her. He was naked but for the thin skin of his traveling armor. Except for claws and teeth, he was unarmed. The vicious gouges across his chest and arms were stained from his pale green blood. And told her he had run afoul of his companions and had been forced out of the pack.

A distraction for her, she imagined, and didn't intend to spend much time dispatching him.

'They sacrificed you,' she said as she circled. 'What was your crime?'

He only hissed, flicking his long tongue through those sharp teeth. She taunted him with a happy grin, muscles ready. Above all else, she lived for combat.

When he leaped, she spun her sword up, down, and severed his head with one smooth stroke. Though the ease of the job was a bit of a disappointment, she grunted in satisfaction as the green blood sizzled and smoked. And the body of the Bok melted away to nothing but an ugly smear on the ground.

'Not much of a challenge,' she muttered and sheathed her sword. 'Still, the day is young, so there is hope for better.'

Her hand was still on the hilt when she heard the scream.

She ran, her dark hair flying behind her, the band of her rank that encircled her head glinting like vengeance. When she burst into the small clearing with its tidy line of huts, she saw that the single Bok had been but a brief distraction, delaying her just long enough.

Bodies of animals and a few men who had tried to defend their homes lay torn and bleeding on the ground. Others were running in panic, some holding their young clutched to them as they scattered. And she knew they would be hunted down and rent to pieces if a single demon escaped her duty.

Sorrow for the dead and the thrill of upcoming battle warred inside her.

Three of the Bok were crouched in the dirt, still feeding. Their eyes glowed red, their vicious teeth snapped as she charged. They sprang, mad enough with blood to choose fight over flight.

She cleaved the arm from one, leaped into a flying kick to knock another out of her way as she plunged her ready dagger into the heart of the third.

'I am Kadra,' she shouted, 'Slayer of Demons. Guardian of the red sun.'

'You are too late,' the remaining Bok hissed at her. 'You are outnumbered. Our king will tear out your heart, and we will share in the feast.'

'Today you go hungry.'

He was faster than the others, and fueled by his grisly meal. This, she knew, would be an opponent more worthy of her skill.

He chose not his claws but the long hooked blade he drew from the sheath at his side.

Steel rang to steel as the screams and the stench rose

around her. She knew there were at least three others and she knew now that the demon king, the one called Sorak, was among them.

His death was her life's work.

The Bok fought well with his sickle sword, and swiped out with those blue claws. She felt the pain, an absent annoyance, as they dug furrows over her bare shoulder. Instead of retreating, she pushed into the attack, into the flashing blue and silver to run him through with a fierce thrust.

'I am Kadra,' she murmured as the Bok smoked to the ground. 'I am your death.'

She wheeled to aim her weapon and her gaze on the demon king and the three warriors that flanked him outside the open doorway of a hut.

At last, she thought. Praise the powers of life, at last.

'I am your death, Sorak,' she said. 'As I was death for Clud, your father. On this day, in this hour, I will rid my world of you.'

'Keep your world.' The king of demons, regal in his red tunic and bands of gold, lifted a small, clear globe. 'I go to another. There I will conquer and feed. There I will rule.'

His handsome face was sheened with sweat and blood. His dark hair coiled, sleek and twisted, like snakes over his elegant shoulders. Then he bared his teeth, and the illusion of rough beauty vanished into horror.

'Where I go, the food is plentiful. There, I will be a god. Keep your world, Kadra, Demon Slayer. Or come with me.' He beckoned with a voice seductive as a caress. 'I will give you the Demon Kiss. I will make you my queen and plant my young inside you. We will rule this new world together.'

'You want to kiss me? To join with me?'

'You have shed the blood of my sire. I have drunk the blood of a slayer. We are well matched. Together we will have power beyond all imagining.'

His three warriors were armed. And a demon king's strength knew no equal among his kind. Four against one, Kadra thought with a leap of her heart. It would be her greatest battle.

'Come, then.' She all but purred it. 'Come embrace me.'

She pursed her own lips, then charged.

To her shock, the demon swirled his cloak, and with his warriors, vanished in a sudden flash of light.

'Where ... how?' She spun in a circle, sword raised, dagger ready, and her blood still singing a war song. She could smell them, a lingering stench. It was all that was left of them.

Women were weeping. Children wailing. And she had

failed. Three Bok, and their hellborn king, had escaped her. Their eyes had met, and yet Sorak had defeated her without landing a blow.

'You have not lost them yet.'

Kadra looked toward the hut where a woman stood in the doorway. She was pale and beautiful, her hair a midnight rain, her face like something carved from delicate glass. But her eyes, green as Kadra's own, were ancient, and in them it seemed worlds could live.

In them, Kadra saw pain.

'Lady,' she said respectfully as she stepped toward her. 'You are injured.'

'I will heal. I know my fate, and it is not time for me to pass.'

'Call the healer,' Kadra told her. 'I must hunt.'

'Yes, you must hunt. Come inside, I will show you how.'

Now Kadra's eyebrows raised. The woman was beautiful, true, and there was an air of magic about her. But she was still only a female.

'I'm a demon slayer. Hunting is what I know.'

'In this world,' the woman agreed. 'But not in the one where you must go. The demon king has stolen one of the keys. But there are others.'

She swayed, and Kadra leaped forward, cursing, to catch

her. Frail bones, she thought. Such delicate bones would shatter easily.

'Why did they let you live?' Kadra demanded as she helped the woman inside.

'It is not in their power to destroy me. To harm, but not to vanquish. I did not know they were coming.' She shook her head as she lowered herself into a chair by a hearth left cold in the heat of day. 'My own complacency blinded me to them. But not to you.' She smiled then, and those eyes were brilliant. 'Not to you, Kadra, Slayer of Demons. I've waited for you.'

'Why?'

'You call me lady, and once I was. Once I was a young girl of rank who took a brave warrior into her heart, and gave him her body in love. He was killed in the Battle of the Singing River.

'It was a great battle against the Bok and the demon tribes who joined them.' Impressed, Kadra tilted her head. She had been weaned on battle stories, and this was the greatest of all. 'Many were destroyed on all sides. Many brave warriors perished, as did three slayers. The numbers of Bok were halved, but still Clud escaped and since increased those numbers again to plague our world.

'I watched the battle in my fire, and in the moment my

love was struck down, in that moment of grief, I bore a girl child. She who was born to take up a sword as her father had done. She who would be more than those who made her. You are she. You are my blood and flesh and bone. I am she who bore you. I am your mother.'

Kadra retreated one step. Where there had been pity was now anger. 'I have no mother.'

'You know I speak true. You have vision enough to see.'

She felt the truth like a burn in the heart, but wanted only to deny it. 'Humans who are not slayers keep their young. They tend and guard and protect them even at the risk of death.'

'So it should be.' The woman's voice thickened with regret. 'I could not keep you with me. My duty was here, holding the keys, and yours was your training. I could not give you a mother's comfort, a mother's care, or a father's pride. Parting with you was another death for me.'

'I need no mother,' Kadra said flatly. 'Nor father. I am a slayer.'

'Yes. This is your fate, and even I could not turn your life's wheel away from it. As I cannot turn it now from where you must go, from what you must do.'

'I must hunt.'

'And you will. Our world and another are at stake. I

could not keep you then,' she stated. 'I cannot keep you now. Though I have never let you go.'

Kadra shook her head. She was accustomed to physical pain, but not to this hurt inside the heart. 'The one who bore me was a warrior, as I am. She died at demon claws when I was but a child.'

'Your foster mother. A good and brave warrior. At her side you learned what you needed to learn. When she was taken from you, you learned more. Now, you will learn the rest. I am Rhee.'

'Rhee.' Kadra, fearless in battle, went pale. 'Rhee is a legend, a sorceress of unspeakable power. She is closed in a crystal mountain, of her own making, and will free herself when the world has need.'

'Stories and tales, with only some truths.' For the first time, Rhee's lips curved in a smile lovely in humor. 'The green of Tulle is my home. No mountain of glass. You have my magic in you, and it is you who must free herself. There is great need. In this world, and the other.'

'What other?' Kadra snapped. 'This *is* the world. The only world.'

'There are more, countless others. The world from which the demons sprang. Worlds of fire, worlds of ice. And a world not so different from this – yet so different. Sorak has gone to this world, through the portal opened by the glass key. He has gone to plunder and kill, to gather power until he is immortal. He wants your blood, wants your death to avenge his father. More, even more, he wants the power he believes he will gain by making you his mate.'

'He will not have me, in this world or any. He would have slain his own father in time if I had not destroyed Clud before him.'

'You see the truth. This is vision.'

'This is sense.'

'Whatever you choose to name it,' Rhee said with a wave of her hand. 'But a king cannot rule without vanquishing his most feared foe. Or changing her. He will not rest until you are destroyed by death or by his kiss. He goes through the portal to begin his own hunt. With every death from demon hands in that place, another here will die. This is the balance. This is the price.'

'You speak in riddles. I will fetch the healer before I hunt.'

'If you turn away,' Rhee said as Kadra got to her feet, 'if you choose the wrong path, all is lost. The world you know, the one you need to know. There is more than one key.' Rhee breathed raggedly as her pain grew, took another clear globe from the folds of her skirt. 'And more than one mirror.'

She waved a hand toward the empty hearth. Fire, bright as gold, leaped into the cold shadow.

In it, Kadra saw another jungle. One of silver and black. Mountains . . . No, structures of great height – surely they could not be huts – rivers of black and white that had no current. Over them great armies of people marched. Over them battalions of animals on four round legs raced.

'What is this place?'

'A great village. They call it a city. A place where people live and work, where they eat and sleep. Where they live and die. This is called New York, and it is there you'll find them. The demons you must stop, and the man who will help you.'

Though fascinated, and just a bit frightened of the images in the flames, Kadra smirked. 'I need no man in battle.'

'So you have been taught,' Rhee said with a smile. 'Perhaps you needed to believe you needed no one, no man, to become what you have become. Now you will become more. To do so, you will need this man. He is called Doyle, Harper Doyle.'

'What good is a harper to a warrior?' Kadra demanded. 'A fine warrior he'll make with his song and story as sword and shield.'

'He is what you need. You will fail without him. Even with him there is great risk.'

15

'Why should I believe any of this? Any witch might conjure pictures in a fire. Any woman might spin a tale as easily as thread.'

'The stone in your crown of rank, those in your sword, I gave to you. For strength, for clear vision, for valor, and last, for love. They were my tears when I gave you to your fate. In my eyes you see your own. In your heart, you see the truth. Now we must prepare.'

Kadra set her hand on the hilt of her sword. 'I am prepared.'

With a heavy sigh, Rhee got to her feet. She walked to a wooden cupboard, took out a metal box. 'Take this.' She offered a bag of stones. 'Where you go,' she explained, 'they have great value.'

Kadra looked into the bag of shining stones. 'Then where I go is a very foolish place.'

'In some ways. In others, fantastic.' Rhee's expression was soft. 'You have much to see. I will give you what knowledge I can, but there are limits. Even for me.' She held out her hands, gripped Kadra's before Kadra could draw back.

'The rest,' she said, and glinting tears scored down her cheeks, 'is up to you, and the man called Doyle.'

A great roar, like rushing water over cliffs, filled Kadra's head. In it were words, a hundred thousand words, spoken in countless tongues. A pressure, as a boulder laid on her heart, filled her chest.

The light was blinding.

'Valor and strength you have, my child. Use them on this journey wild. But open yourself to vision, to love, before it's too late. Gather them close and face your fate. Would I could keep you safe with me,' she murmured, and her lips brushed a kiss over Kadra's. 'But once again I set you free.'

The world whirled and spun. The air sucked her in, tumbled her, then spat her rudely out.

2

Sprawled in bed, plagued by the mother of all hangovers, the man called Doyle let out a surprised and pained grunt when a half-naked woman dropped on top of him.

He saw eyes of intense and burning green. Eyes, he thought blearily, that he'd been dreaming of moments before he'd awakened with a head the size of Nebraska.

There was an instant of recognition, a strange and intimate knowledge, and with it a bone-deep longing. Then there was nothing but shock. .

He had time to blink, a split second to admire what he was certain was a very creative hallucination, before the very sharp and very real point of a dagger pressed against his carotid artery.

'I am Kadra,' the mostly naked and well-armed hallucination stated in a throaty voice as oddly familiar as her eyes. 'Slayer of Demons.'

'Okay, that's really interesting.' If he'd been drunk and stupid enough the night before to bring a crazy woman back to his apartment, and couldn't even remember heating up the sheets with her, he deserved to get his throat cut.

But it really wasn't the way he wanted to start the day.

'Would you mind getting that pig-sticker away from my jugular? You're spoiling a perfectly good hangover.'

Frowning, she sniffed at him, then used her free hand to pull up his top lip and study his teeth. Satisfied, she drew back the dagger, slid it handily into its wrist sheath.

'You are not a demon. You may live.'

'Appreciate it.' Going with instinct rather than sanity, Harper shoved her, snatched at the dagger. The next thing he knew, she'd executed a neat back flip off the bed, landed on her feet beside it. With a very big sword raised over her head.

'You win.' He tossed the dagger aside, held up both hands.

'You yield?'

'Damn right. Why don't you put that thing down before somebody – especially me – gets hurt? Then we can go call the nice people at the asylum. They'll come pick you up and take you for a little ride.'

Disgusted that she'd landed on a coward, she shook her head. But she lowered the sword. 'Are you the harper called Doyle?'

'I'm Harper Doyle.'

'We have to hunt.'

'Sure, no problem.' Smiling at her, he eased toward the far side of the bed. Whatever that feeling had been when he'd first looked into her eyes, he was sure now he hadn't been drunk enough, hadn't been stupid enough to bring her home with him. 'Just let me get my hunting gear and we'll be off.'

Using his body to block her view, he slid open the drawer in the nightstand and drew out his Glock. 'Now, put that goddamn sword down, Xena.'

'I am Kadra,' she corrected and studied the object in his hand. 'This is a gun.' The name, the purpose of it were floating in her head, in the maze of knowledge Rhee had given her. The fascination for it, this new weapon, made her yearn. 'I would like to have one.'

She looked at him, studying his face for the first time, and found herself shocked that it brought her another kind of yearning.

'I was sent to you,' she told him.

'Fine, we'll get to that. But right now, put the sword down,' he repeated. 'I'd really hate to spoil my record and shoot a woman.'

It was more comfortable to study the gun, and her feelings for an interesting weapon. 'The missile goes through flesh and bone. It can be very efficient.' She nodded, sent her sword home. 'Perhaps you are a warrior. We will talk.'

'Oh, yeah,' Harper agreed. 'We're going to have a very nice chat.'

His head felt as if someone had spent the night attempting a lobotomy with a dull, rusty blade. He could accept that. In a bemused celebration of his thirtieth birthday – how could he be thirty when he'd been eighteen two minutes ago – he'd consumed a tanker truck of alcohol. He'd been entitled to get plastered with a couple of pals. He was entitled to the hangover.

Having a woman – a gorgeous green-eyed Amazon who filled out her black leather bikini in a way that gratified every young boy's comic book fantasies – leap on him out of nowhere was a really nice plus. Just the sort of happy birthday surprise a man who'd reached the point of no return on the path to adulthood could appreciate.

But having that erotic armful hold a knife to his throat wasn't part of the acceptable package.

And where the hell *had* she come from? he wondered as she stood there eyeing his gun. There was nothing but simple curiosity and avid interest on that sharp-boned siren's face.

Had he been so drunk he'd forgotten to lock his door? It was a possibility – a remote one, but a possibility. But she'd called him by name. No way she was from the neighborhood. He was a trained observer, and even if he'd been a myopic accountant rather than a private investigator he would have noticed a six-foot brunette with legs that went to eternity.

'Jake.' The solution trickled through his suffering brain. Though he relaxed a little, he held the gun steady. 'Jake put you up to this, didn't he? Some weird-ass birthday surprise. Jake's who sent you.'

'I am sent by Rhee, the sorceress. How is it that a harper has such a weapon? Have you killed many demons?'

'Look, it's too early in the morning for Dungeons and Dragons. Show's over, sister.'

'I am not your sister,' she began as he eased out of bed.

Then her eyebrows shot up. He was naked, but that neither surprised nor shocked her. Her instant and elemental attraction did.

He was taller than she by nearly a full hand, broader in the chest and shoulders, with fine, sleek muscles.

Reevaluating, she pursed her lips. His hair was the deep brown of oak bark, and though unkempt by sleep, it created a good frame for a strong face. His eyes were the bold blue of the marsh bells, his nose slightly crooked, which told her it had weathered a break. His mouth was firm, as was his jaw. Though his skin was pale, like a scholar's who closeted himself with scrolls, she began to see possibilities.

'You have a fine build for a harper,' she told him.

'Yeah?' Amused now, though still cautious, he reached for the jeans he'd peeled off the night before. 'How much did Jake pay you for the gig?'

'I know no Jake. I do not take payment for slaying. It is my destiny. Do you require payment?'

'Depends.' How the hell was he going to get into his jeans and hold the gun at the same time?

'The knowledge was given me that these have value in your world.' She tugged the bag of stones from her belt, tossed them on the bed. 'Take what you need, then dress. We must begin the hunt.'

'Look, I appreciate a joke as much as the next guy. But I'm naked and hungover, and it irritates me to wake up with a knife to my throat. I want coffee, a barrel of aspirin, and a shower.'

'Very well. If you will not hunt, show me how to use your weapon.'

'You're a piece of work.' He gestured toward the bedroom door with the Glock. 'Out. Back to Central Casting, or Amazons R Us, or wherever the hell—'

She moved so fast that all he saw was a blur of limbs and leather and flying hair. She leaped, executed a handspring off the bed, and some part of her – boot, elbow, fist – connected with his jaw.

An entire galaxy of stars exploded in his head. By the time they novaed and died, he was flat on his back, with her standing astride him turning the Glock over in her hands.

'It has good weight,' she said conversationally. 'How is the missile . . . ' She trailed off when with a twitch of her finger she fired. Her eyes widened with something like lust when through the open bathroom door, she saw the corner of his vanity sheared off.

'It is faster than an arrow,' she commented, very pleased.

Not Jake, he corrected. Jake might have a weird sense of the ridiculous, but his old college friend wouldn't have sent him a lunatic who liked to play with guns. 'Who the hell are you?'

'I am Kadra.' She nearly sighed with the repetition – perhaps the harper was loose in the brains. With some sympathy she offered a hand to help him up. 'Slayer of Demons. I have come to hunt, to fulfill my destiny. Though it does not please either of us, you are obliged to assist.'

'Give me the gun, Kadra.'

'It is a good weapon.'

'Yeah, it's a good weapon. It belongs to me.'

Her lips moved into a pout, then her face brightened again. 'I will fight you for it.'

'I'm at a disadvantage at the moment.' He got to his feet, very slowly, kept his voice mild and easy. 'You know, naked, hungover.'

'Hung over what?'

'Maybe we could fight later, after we clear up a few points.'

'Very well. I will give you the weapon, and you will give me your word that you will help me hunt the Bok.'

'Helping people's what I do.' Maybe she was in trouble, he thought. Not that he intended to get involved, but he could at least listen before he called the guys in the white coats. 'Is that why you're here?' Gently, he nudged her gun hand aside so he wouldn't end up with a bullet in the belly. 'You need help?'

'I am a stranger here, and require a guide.' She reached out, squeezed his biceps. 'You are strong. But slow.' With no little regret, she returned the Glock. 'Can you make more of the gun?'

'Maybe.' She'd threatened him with a knife, with a sword. She'd knocked him on his ass and disarmed him.

Damn if he didn't respect her for it.

In any case, she'd made his first morning as a thirty-year-old man interesting. He hadn't become a PI because he liked the boring.

Added to that, there was something . . . something about her that pulled at him. Her looks were enough to knock a man flat. But it wasn't that – or not only that. You couldn't find the answers, he reminded himself, unless you asked the questions.

'I'm going to put my pants on,' he told her. 'I want you to step back and keep your hands away from that sword.'

She stepped back. 'I have no wish to harm you, or any of your people. You have my word as a slayer.'

'Good to know.' When she was at a safe distance, he tugged on his jeans, then snugged the gun in the waistband. 'Now, I'm going to make coffee, and we'll talk about all this.'

'Coffee. This is a stimulant consumed in liquid form.'

'There you go. In the kitchen,' he added, gesturing toward the door.

She strode out ahead of him. Whatever shape he might have been in, Harper thought, however baffled he might be, a man who didn't admire and appreciate that view was a sorry specimen.

Still, he glanced at the front door of his apartment as he passed. It was locked, bolted, chained.

So she'd locked up after she'd come in, he decided. He looked back to see her stop and gape out the living room window. Like a kid might, he mused, at her first eyeful of Disneyland.

So high, she thought in wonder. She had never been in a hut where the ground was so far below and so many people swarmed beneath. Their costumes were strange to her, strange and fascinating. But fascination turned to awe when she watched a cab zip to the curb, saw the woman leap out.

'She rose out of the belly of the yellow beast! How is this done?'

'You pay the fare, they let you out. Where the hell are you from?'

'I am from A'Dair. In my world, we have no beasts with

round legs. I don't – wait.' She closed her eyes, searched through the knowledge Rhee had given her. 'Cars!' Those brilliant eyes opened again, smiled into his. 'They are machines called cars and are for transportation. That is wonderful.'

'Try to find one in the rain. Honey—'

'Yes, I would like honey, and bread. I am hungry.'

'Right.' He shook his head. 'Coffee. Coffee first, then all questions can be faced. Come with me. I want you where I can see you.'

She followed him into his tiny galley kitchen. While he measured coffee, she ran her fingers over the surface of the counter, over the refrigerator and stove. 'So much magic,' she said softly. 'You must have great wealth.'

'Yeah, rolling in it.' He made a reasonable living, Harper thought. But he was what you could call between active cases at the moment. Maybe he could hold off on the guys in the white coats, see if she needed an investigator, and had enough to pay his retainer. 'Jake didn't send you, did he?'

'I do not know this Jake.' She peered at the side of the toaster, delighted with her own odd reflection. 'I know no one in this world, save you.'

'How did you get here, to my place?'

'Through the portal. It is . . . ' She straightened, trying to decipher the knowledge, then to express it. 'There are many dimensions. Yours and mine are two. The Bok stole a key and have entered yours. I have another.' She drew the clear globe out of her pouch. 'So I have followed. To hunt, to kill so that our worlds will be safe. You are to help me in this quest.'

Poor kid, he thought. She was definitely a few fries short of a Happy Meal. 'You can't just kill people in this world. They lock you up for that.'

'You have no slayers to fight against evil here?'

He dragged a hand through his hair, then rooted out some Extra-Strength Excedrin. Isn't that what his father had done? And what he himself had wanted to do as long as he could remember? To go after the bad guys, on his own terms?

'Yeah, I guess we do.'

The woman was definitely in some sort of jam, even if it came out of her own oddball imagination. He would just keep her calm, ask some questions, see if he could dig out the problem. When he'd done what he could, he would make a few calls and have her taken someplace where she could get some help.

It would be the first good deed of his new decade.

'So, you come from another dimension, and you're here to hunt down some demons.'

'The king of demons and three of his warriors have entered your world. They will need to feed. First, they will hunt for animals, the easy kill, to gather strength. Where are your farms?'

'We're a little short on farms on Second Avenue. So what do you do back in – where was it?'

'A'Dair.'

He could run a search on the name on his computer, see if he could pinpoint where she'd come from. She didn't have a discernible accent, but the cadence, the rhythm of her speech sure as hell didn't say New York.

'What do you do back in A'Dair besides slay demons?'

'This is my purpose. I was born a slayer, trained, educated. It is what I do.'

'Friends, family?'

'I have no family. She who raised me was killed by a tribe of Bok.'

Mother killed, he thought. Trauma, role playing. 'I'm sorry.'

'She was a fine warrior. Clud, sire of Sorak, took her life, and I have taken his. So there is balance. I have learned that she who bore me was another. Rhee, the sorceress. Her blood is in me. I think I am here, able to be here, because of that blood.' She sniffed the air. 'This is coffee?'

'That's right.'

'It has a good scent.'

He poured two mugs, offered one. She sniffed again, sipped, then frowned. 'Bitter, but good.'

To his surprise, she downed the entire mug in one swallow, then swiped a hand over her mouth. 'I like this coffee. Dress now, Harper Doyle.'

'How do you know my name?'

'It was told to me. We will hunt the Bok together.'

'Sure. We'll get to that in a little while.'

Her eyes narrowed. 'You don't believe. You think I'm loose in the brain. You waste my time with too many questions when we should act.'

'Part of what I do in my little world is ask questions. Nobody's calling you a liar here. Why shouldn't I believe you're a demon slayer from an alternate universe? I'm always getting clients from other dimensions.'

She paced up and down the narrow room to work out the logic. He was mocking her, and this was not proper. Lesser warriors were not permitted to show a slayer disrespect.

Yet, she admired him for it even as she found his demeanor frustrating.

This was his world, Kadra reminded herself, one of wonders far beyond her ken. So her world would be beyond his.

If she were in his place, she would not believe without proof.

'You must be shown. I cannot blame you for doubt. You would be weak and foolish if you didn't question, and the weak and foolish would be of no use to me.'

'Darling, keep up that sweet talk and you'll turn my head.'

She didn't have to understand the words to recognize the sarcasm dripping from them. A little impatient, a little intrigued, she held one hand up, and the other, with the globe in its palm, out.

'My blood is of the sorceress and the warrior. My blood is the blood of the slayer. I hold the power of the key.'

She drew her mind down to the globe, drew the power of the globe into her mind.

Harper's kitchen wall dissolved as though it were a painting left out in the rain. Through it, he saw not the apartment next door but a thick, green jungle, a curving white ribbon, and a sky the color of pale blood under a fierce red sun.

'Holy shit,' he managed before he was sucked into it.

3

The heat was enormous, a drenching, dripping wall of steaming water. It was a shock, even after the jolt of pain, the blast of blinding light. Even so, his bones felt frozen under his skin as he stared out at the tangle of towering green.

New York was gone, it seemed. And so was he.

Not a hangover, he thought, but some sort of psychotic event brought on, no doubt, by too much liquor and too many loose women.

As he watched, dumbfounded, a snake with a body as thick as his thigh slithered off into the high, damp grass.

'We can stay only a short time,' Kadra told him, and her voice was dim, tinny, light-years away. 'This is the west jungle of A'Dair, near the coast of the Great Sea. This is my world, which exists beyond yours. And the knowledge says, in balance with it.'

'I've been drugged.'

'This is not so.' Annoyed now, she clamped her hands over his arms. 'You can see, you can hear and feel. My world is as real as yours, and as much in peril.'

'Alternate universe.' The words felt foolish on his tongue. 'That's pure science fiction.'

'Is your world so perfect, so important, that you believe it stands alone in the vastness of time and space? Harper Doyle, can you have lived and still believe you are alone? My heart.' She pressed his hand to her breast. 'It beats as yours. I am, as you are.'

How could he dismiss what he saw with his own eyes. What he felt, touched — and somehow knew. Just, he thought, as he had somehow known her the instant their eyes had met. 'Why?'

She nearly smiled. 'Why not?'

'I recognized you,' he managed. 'I pushed that aside,

clicked back into what made sense so I could deny it. But I recognized you, somehow, the minute I saw you.'

'Yes.' She kept her hand on his a moment longer. It felt right there, like a link. 'It was the same for me. This is not something I understand, but only feel. I do not know the meaning.'

And in some secret chamber of her warrior's heart, she feared the meaning.

'I'm standing here sweating in a jungle in some Twilight Zone, and it doesn't feel half as strange as it should. It doesn't feel half as strange as what's going on inside me, about you.'

'You begin to believe.'

'I'm beginning to something. I'm going to need a little time to process all the—'

She whirled, the sword streaking into her hand like a lightning bolt. A creature, no more than three feet high, with snapping teeth in both its mouths, shot out of the brush and leaped for Harper's throat.

Despite the shock of it, his instincts were quick. His hand whipped down for his gun. It hadn't cleared the waistband of his jeans before Kadra's sword sliced through both heads with one massive stroke. There was a fountaining gush of vile green liquid that stank like sulfur.

Heads and body thunked, a grisly trio, onto the ground, then began to smoke.

'Loki demon,' Kadra said as the three pieces melted away. 'Small pests that usually travel in packs of three.' She lifted her head, sniffed. 'To your left. You will need your weapon,' she added, and pivoted to her right as another of the creatures jumped through a curtain of vine.

Instinct had his finger on the trigger, and if that finger trembled a bit, he wasn't ashamed. He heard the slice of her sword through air just as the last – please, God – of the miniature monsters charged him.

He shot it between the eyes – all four of them.

'Christ. Jesus. Christ.'

'This is good aim.' Giving Harper a congratulatory slap on the back, she nodded over the smoking heads. 'This is a fine weapon,' she added, sending his Glock an avaricious glance. 'When we go back to your world, you will provide me with one. It lacks the beauty of the sword, but it makes an enjoyable noise.'

'Their blood's green,' Harper said in a careful voice. 'They have two heads and green blood. And now, how about that, they're just melting away like the Wicked Witch of the West.'

'All demons bleed green, though only the Loki and the mutant strain of the Ploon are two-headed. On death, the blood smokes and the body . . . melts is not inaccurate,' she decided. 'You have witches in the west of your world who die like demons?'

When he only stared at her, she shrugged. 'We have witches as well, and most of them the powers of life have instilled with good. My home is east,' she continued. 'Beyond the Stone Mountains, in the Shadowed Valley. It is beautiful, and the fields are rich. There is no time to show you.'

'This is real.' He took one long, deep breath and swallowed it all at once.

'Our time here is short. There is a clearing, and a village in it. Rhee lives there. We will go.'

Since she set off in a punishing jog, he had no choice but to follow. 'Slow it down, Wonder Woman. I'm barefoot here.'

She tossed a scowl over her shoulder, but modified her pace. 'You drank excessive spirits last night. I can smell them on you. Now you are sluggish.'

'Alert enough to kill a two-headed demon.'

She let out a snort. 'A child with a training bow could do the same. Lokis are stupid.'

As they ran down the narrow, beaten path, a flock of birds flushed out of the trees and into that odd red sky. He staggered to a halt. Each was its own rainbow – a bleeding, blending meld of pinks and blues and golds. And the song they sent up was like the trill of flutes.

'Dregos,' she told him. 'Their gift is their song, as they are poor eating. Stringy.' She slowed to a trot as they came to the clearing.

He saw houses, small and tidy, most with colorful gardens in the front. People dressed in long, thin robes harvested out of them what looked to be massive blue carrots, tomatoes the size of melons, and long, yellow beans spotted with green flecks.

There were men, women, children, and each stopped work or play and bowed as Kadra came into view.

'Greetings, Demon Slayer,' some called out.

She acknowledged this with what Harper supposed was a kind of salute by laying her fist on her heart as she walked.

Those long legs ate up the ground toward a small house with a lush garden and an open front door. She had to duck her head to enter.

Inside, a young girl stood by what he assumed was a cookstove. She stirred an iron pot and looked up at them with quiet blue eyes.

'Hail to Kadra, Slayer of Demons.'

'We come to speak with Rhee.'

'She sleeps,' the girl said and continued to stir. 'She suffered a demon bite during the attack.'

'She did not say.' Kadra moved quickly, shoving open a door. Within, Rhee lay pale and still on a bed. The emotions that churned in her were mixed and confusing, and through them came one clear thought.

Mother. Will I lose yet another mother before my own end? 'Is it the sleep of change?'

'No. She was not kissed, only bitten beneath the shoulder as she tried to guard the keys. Nor was it a mortal bite, though she had pain and there was sickness. More than necessary, as she did not see to the wound quickly.'

'She . . . spent too much time with me.'

'Not too much, only what was needed.'

'Your mother?' Harper looked through the doorway at the woman on the bed, and laid a hand on Kadra's shoulder. 'Can we get her to a doctor?'

'I am Mav the healer,' the young girl told him. 'I tend to her. I have drained the poison, given her the cure. She must sleep until her body regains strength. She said you would come, Kadra, with the one from the other world. You are to eat.'

Mav ladled out some of the thick broth from the pot. 'And to wash in the falls. In this way, you will take some of this place with you into the next. You must be gone within the hour.'

'Do you want to sit with her awhile,' Harper began. 'Take some time with her?'

His hand caressed her shoulder, a gesture of comfort she had known rarely in her life. 'There is no time.' Kadra turned away from the doorway.

'She's your mother.'

'She bore me. She set me on this path. Now I can only follow it.'

She sat down at the table where Mav had put the bowls and a round loaf of golden bread. There was a squat pitcher of honey and another of water as white and sparkling as snow.

Because he was tired, hungry, and confused, Harper sat. This is real, he thought again as he sampled the first taste of the rich, spiced broth. It wasn't a dream, a hallucination. He hadn't just lost his mind.

Kadra tore off a hunk of bread, poured honey over it, and ate with a concentrated focus that told Harper she wasn't concerned with taste, only with fuel.

'Do you have family?' she asked Mav between bites.

'I have two brothers, younger. My mother who weaves. My father was a healer as well. Sorak, king of demons, killed him this morning.'

'I was not quick enough.' Grief thickened Kadra's voice. 'And your mother is a widow.'

'He would have killed us all, but you came. He fears you.'

'He has cause. I regret that death touched you.'

'He came for Rhee, for the key. Her powers are not as strong as they were, and he made demons from wizards so he might track her. She explained to me while I tended her so I might tell you.'

Mav folded her hands and spoke as if reciting a story learned by heart. 'The other, the world beyond with yellow sun and blue sky, is full of so much life, and most who live there have closed themselves off from the magic. They will not understand, they will not believe, and so the Bok will slaughter them. Flesh, passion. Innocence and evil. Sorak craves this, and the power he will gain from it. The power to destroy you.'

'He will die there.' Kadra drank the tankard of spring-water quickly. 'This is my vow, on your father's blood.' She pulled out her dagger, sliced a shallow gash across her palm, and let her blood drip onto the table. 'And on mine.'

'It will comfort my mother to know it. But there should be no more bloodshed here.' Mav reached in her pocket, took out a white cloth, and deftly wrapped it around Kadra's hand. 'You must wash in the falls, for cleansing, then go.'

When Kadra got to her feet, Harper sighed and got to his. 'Thanks for the food.'

Mav blushed, cast down her gaze. 'It is little to give the Slayer and the savior. Blessings on you both.'

Harper took one last glance at her. Kid couldn't be more than ten, he thought, then ducked out the doorway.

He had to double his pace to catch up with Kadra. 'Look, just slow down a minute. I'm trying to keep up here, in more ways than one. I don't usually spend my mornings visiting alternate dimensions and killing loco demons.'

'Loki.'

'Whatever. So far you've jumped me, held a knife to my throat, threatened me with a sword, punched me in the face, and sucked me through some . . . wormhole in my kitchen. And all this on one lousy cup of coffee. This isn't your average first date.'

'You do not have the knowledge, so you require explanations.' She moved through the jungle at a brisk pace, eyes tracking, ears pricked. 'I understand this.'

'Beautiful. Then give them to me.'

'We will cleanse in the falls, return to your world, hunt down the Bok and kill them.'

He considered himself a reasonable guy, a man with an open mind, an active sense of adventure and curiosity. But enough was enough. He grabbed her arm, yanked her around to face him. 'That's what you call an explanation? Listen, sister, if that's the best you can do, this is where we part ways. Send me back where I come from and we'll just put this all down to too much beer and fried food.'

'I am not your sister.'

He stared at her, at the faint irritation that clouded her glorious face. Helpless, he began to laugh. It rolled out of him, pumping up from the belly so that he had to bend over, brace his hands on his thighs as she cocked her head and studied him with a mixture of amusement, puzzlement, and impatience.

'I'm losing it,' he managed. 'Losing what's left of my mind.' Even as he sucked in a breath, a spider the size of a Chihuahua pranced between his feet on stiltlike legs and gibbered at him. Harper yelped, whipping out his gun as he stumbled back.

But Kadra merely booted the enormous insect off the path. 'That species is not poisonous,' she informed him.

'Good, great, fine! It just swallows a man whole.'

Kadra shook her head, then loped down the path. Keeping his gun handy, Harper followed.

Red sun, he mused as he looked up at the sky. Like, well, Krypton. If he followed comic book logic, didn't that mean that he, from a planet with a yellow sun, had superpowers here.

Concentrating, he took a little jump, then another. On the third, Kadra looked back at him, her face a study in baffled frustration. 'This is not the time for dancing.'

'I wasn't dancing I was just . . . ' Seeing if I could fly, he thought, amazed at himself. 'Nothing. Nothing at all.'

He heard the roar like a highballing train. It grew, swelled, pounded on his eardrums as he jogged after her. She swung around a curve on the path, and he looked up.

In front of them, white water plunged from a height of two hundred feet or more. It screamed over the cliff, dived in a thundering wall, then pounded into the surface of a white river.

Flowers, some unrecognizable, some as simple as daisies, teemed along its banks. There, with the wild grass and wild-flowers, with the sunlight spilling in rosy streaks through the canopy of trees, a unicorn lazily grazed.

'My God.' The hand still holding the gun fell to his side. The mythical beast raised its regal white head and stared at Harper out of eyes so blue and clear they might have been glass. Then it went back to cropping the grass.

The beauty of it, the sheer wonder, wiped his temper away. Now I've seen it all, he thought. Nothing will ever surprise me again.

He realized the fallacy of that a second later when he glanced back at Kadra.

She'd stripped. The black leather lay piled on the bank, her sword, her dagger crossed over it. She'd pulled off her boots, her wrist sheaths, and was even now reaching up to lift the circlet from her hair.

She was, Harper thought, more mythical, more wondrous that the white-horned creature. Her body was curved and sleek, the color of the fresh honey she had poured over the breakfast bread. Her dark hair, arrow straight, rained over her shoulders, down her back, lay tauntingly over one magnificent breast.

His body tightened, his mouth went dry. For one blissful moment, he lost the power of speech.

'This is a sacred place,' she began as she laid her circlet on her crossed blades. 'No demon can cross its borders. Take off your clothing, put down your weapon. You may take no cloth or metal into the falls.'

So saying, she dived.

It was a picture he knew would remain etched in his mind forever.

'Things are looking up,' he decided, and peeling off his jeans, he jumped in after her.

The water was cool, sluicing the sweat from his body in

one glorious swipe. When he surfaced, he felt the last nasty dregs of the morning's hangover sink to the bottom of the river. In fact, he realized as he struck out after Kadra and the falls, he didn't just feel clearheaded, didn't just feel good. He felt charged, energized.

She waited for him at the foot of the falls, treading the churning water lazily. Her eyes were impossibly green, impossibly brilliant.

'What's in this water?' he shouted.

'Cleansing properties. It washes away negative energies.'

'I'll say.'

She laughed, did a quick surface dive that gave him a brief and wonderful flash of her butt. Then she rose again, a vision of black and gold, under the pounding spill of the water. She climbed nimbly onto a plateau of rock, stretched her arms wide to the sides, and let the water beat over her.

He lost his breath, and despite the cool relief of the water, his blood ran hot. He hoisted himself up in front of her, laid his hands on her hips. Her eyes opened again, and her eyebrow quirked.

'You're the most magnificent thing I've ever seen. In any dimension.'

'I have a good build,' she said easily. 'It's made for fighting.' She bent her right arm, flexed her biceps.

'I bet it holds its own in other sports.'

Though she couldn't ignore the trip of her own heart, or the quick click of response in her belly, she only smiled. 'I enjoy sporting, when there's time for such things. You're very handsome, Harper Doyle, and I have a yearning for you that is stronger than any I have known before.'

'Do you think you could pick one of my two names and stick with it?' Since she didn't seem to object, he slid his hands around her thighs, then over her silky butt.

'Harper is your title.'

'No, it's my name. My first name.' He really had to get a taste of that lush, frowning mouth. But as he dipped his head, she laid a restraining hand on his chest.

'I do not understand. Are you the harper called Doyle?'

'I'm Harper Doyle, and before this turns into a comedy routine, Doyle is my family name. Harper is the name my parents gave me when I was born. That's how it works in my world. I'm not *a* harper,' he added as the light began to dawn. 'I'm not, what, like a minstrel? Jesus. I'm a PI.'

'A pee-eye? What is this?'

'Investigator. Private investigator. I . . . solve puzzles,' he decided.

'Ah! You are a seeker. This is better. A seeker is more useful on a hunt than a harper.'

'Now that we've worked that out, why don't we go back to me being handsome.' He drew her closer so that her breasts – cool, wet, firm – brushed his chest. His mouth was an inch from hers when he went flying.

He landed clumsily, swallowing water on his own curse. She was still on the rocks when he came up and swiped the hair out of his eyes. She was grinning. 'You made a good splash. It is time to go.'

She dived, struck out for the bank. Oh, he was handsome, she thought as she hoisted herself out. Very handsome, and with a clever look in his eyes that made her want to join her body to his.

Something about him was making pricks on her heart, as if trying to find the weakness, the point of entry.

He would be a strong lover, she knew. And it had been a long time since she had desired one. If time and fate allowed, they would have each other.

But first, there was the hunt.

By the time he pulled himself onto the bank put on his jeans, she was strapping on her sword. He didn't bother to think, just went with the moment. And tackled her.

She let out a surprised little grunt and studied his face with some approval. 'I misjudged. You do have speed.'

'Yeah, right, it'll help on the hunt. But right now . . .'

He lowered his head, all but tasting that beautiful mouth. And once more he went flying. But this time it was through the portal. The blast of light, and sharp, shocking pain.

He landed hard, with Kadra once more on top, on his kitchen floor. 'Damn it!' He banged his head sharply on the base cabinet, felt the unmistakable shape of his gun dig into his bare back. 'Give me some warning next time. A damn signal or something.'

'You have your mind too much on sporting.' She gave his shoulder a pat, then levered off him. Sniffed the air. 'We will have more coffee, and plan the hunt.'

'Okay, Sheena, let's reevaluate,' he said as he got up.

'I am Kadra—'

'Shut up.' He slapped the gun down on the kitchen counter while her mouth dropped open.

'You would speak so to a slayer?'

'Yeah, I'd speak so to anybody who busts uninvited into my house and keeps giving me orders. You want my help, you want my cooperation? Then you can just stop telling me what to do and start asking.'

She was silent for a moment. She had a ready temper, something even her intense training hadn't completely tamed. To lose it now, she told herself, would be gratifying, but a sinful waste of time. Instead, she measured Harper, then nodded with sudden understanding. 'Ah. You're talking with your man-thing. This is a common ailment in my world as well.'

'This isn't my dick talking.' Or at least, he'd be damned if he'd admit it. 'I want answers. The way I see it, you're looking to hire me. That's fine. You want me to help you track down these . . . things. That's what I do. I find things, solve problems. That's my job. I work my way. Let's get that part straight.'

'You are a seeker, and you require payment. Very well.' Though she thought less of him for it, she wouldn't begrudge him his fee. 'Come with me.' She started out, turned when she saw him standing firm. 'If you will,' she added.

'Better,' he muttered, and followed her into the bedroom, where she scooped up the leather pouch she'd tossed on the bed earlier.

'Is this enough?'

He caught the bag when she flipped it to him. Curious, he opened it. And poured a storm of gems onto the bed. 'Holy Mother of God!'

'I am told these have value here. Is this so?' Intrigued, she stepped over to poke a finger into the pool of diamonds, rubies, emeralds. 'They are common stones in my world.

Pretty,' she admitted. 'Attractive for adornments. Will they satisfy your needs?'

'Satisfy my needs,' he grumbled. 'Yeah, they're pretty satisfactory.'

He could retire. Move to Tahiti and live like a king. Hell, he could *buy* Tahiti and live like a god. For one outrageous moment, he saw himself living in a white palace by the crystal blue water, surrounded by gorgeous, scantily clad women eager to do his bidding. Drinking champagne by the gallons. Frolicking on white sand beaches with those same women – not clad at all now.

Master of all he surveyed.

Then his conscience kicked in, a small annoyance he'd never been able to shake. On the heels of conscience nipped the lowering admission that the fantasy he'd just outlined would bore him brainless in a week.

He picked a single diamond, comforting himself that it was worth more than he would earn in a decade.

'This'll cover it.'

'That is all you require?'

'Put the rest away, before I change my mind.' For lack of a better option, he stuffed the stone into his pocket. 'Now, we're going to sit down. You're going to explain this whole demon deal to me, and I'll figure out our first move.'

'They are out in your world. We have to hunt.'

'My world,' Harper agreed. 'My turf. I don't go after any-thing until I know the score.' He walked to his dresser, opened a drawer, and pulled out a T-shirt. 'Normally I don't meet clients at home,' he said as he pulled the shirt on. 'But we'll make an exception. Living room.' He headed out, took a legal pad from a desk drawer, then plopped down on the sofa.

However fantastic the client, however strange the case, he was going to approach it as he would any other. He made a few notes, then jerked his chin at a chair when she con-tinued to stand. 'Sit down. Bok demon, right? Is that B-O-K? Never mind. How many?'

'They were four. Sorak, demon king, and three warriors.'

'Description?'

She sprawled in a chair, all legs and attitude. He looked more scholar than warrior now, working with his odd scroll and quill. Though she had never found scholar appealing before, this aspect of him was attractive to her as well.

He has brains as well as muscle, she thought. Intellect as well as brawn.

'Description,' Harper repeated. 'What do they look like?'

'They are deceptively human in appearance, and so often walk among people without detection. They are handsome, as you are. Though you have eyes blue as the marsh bell, and your hair is cropped short. Those who are foolish enough to be influenced by such things as beauty are easy victims.'

'We've established that you're nobody's victim, baby. Be more specific.'

She huffed. 'They have good height, like you, but their build is less. It is more . . . slender. Hair and eyes are dark, black as a dead moon except in feeding or in attack, where they glow red.'

'Glowing red eyes,' he noted. 'I'd say that's a fairly distinguishing mark.'

'Sorak's hair curls.' She demonstrated by waving a finger. 'And is well groomed. He is vain.'

'They outfitted like you?'

It took her a moment, then she glanced down at her hunting clothes. 'No. They wear a kind of armor, black again, close to the body, and over this Sorak wears the tunic and cloak of his rank.'

'Even in New York, body armor and tunics should stand out. Maybe there's something on the news.' He picked up the remote and flipped on the television.

Kadra leaped up as if he'd set her chair on fire. Even before her feet were planted, her sword was out, raised high above her head in preparation for a downward thrust.

'Hold it, hold it, hold it!' He jumped and, as he might have done to save a beloved child, threw himself between the blade and his TV. 'I don't give a rat's ass about what you did to the bathroom sink, but put one scratch on my TV and you're going down.'

Her heart pounded in her chest, and her muscles quivered. 'What is this sorcery?'

'It's not magic, it's ESPN.' He hissed out a breath, then moved in to clamp his hands over hers on the hilt of the sword. She tipped her head back so their eyes, their mouths, lined up.

'It's television, which is arguably the national religion of my country. An entertainment device,' he said more calmly. 'A kind of communication. We have programs – ah, like plays, I guess, that tell us what's happening in the world, even when it's happening far away.'

She drew a breath, slowly lowered the sword while she stared at the picture box where the machines called cars ran swiftly around a circle. 'How is this done?'

'Something about airwaves, transmissions, cameras, stuff. Hell, I don't know. You turn the thing on, pick a channel. This is a race. You get that?'

'Yes, a contest of speed. I have won many races.'

'With those legs, baby, I'll just bet you have. Okay, I'm

turning on the news now so we can see if there are any reports on your demons. So relax.'

'How can you use a thing when you have no knowledge of its workings?'

'Same way I can use a computer. And don't ask. I thought you said you knew about this world.'

'I was given knowledge, but I cannot learn it all at once.' It embarrassed her not to know, so she went back to sprawling in the chair, giving the television quick, suspicious glances.

'All right, we'll take it in stages. Just don't attack any more of my household appliances.' He sat again, flipped the channel to the all-news station, then picked up his pad. 'Back to your demons. Distinguishing marks? You know, like two heads, for instance?'

Feeling foolish, she sulked. He had nearly slain a spider with the weapon known as gun, but she had not made *him* feel loose in the brain. 'They are Bok, not Loki.'

'What makes them stand out? How do you recognize them?' Even as she threw up her hands, he tapped his pencil. 'And don't say they are Bok. Draw me a picture.'

Taking him literally, she reared up, snatched the pencil and pad. In fast, surprisingly deft strokes, she sketched a figure of a man with long, curled hair, a strong, rawboned face and large, dark eyes.

'That's good. But it's going to be tough to pick him out of the millions of other tall, slim, dark-haired guys in New York. Doesn't shout out demon to me. How do you recognize them — as a species, let's say.'

'A slayer is born for this. But others might do so by their stench. They have a scent.' She struggled for a moment in her attempt to describe it. 'Between the ripe and the rot. You would not mistake it.'

'Okay, they stink. Now we're getting somewhere. Anything else?'

'Teeth. Two rows, long, thin, sharp. Claws, which they show or conceal at will. Thick, blue, curved like talons. And when they are wounded, their blood is green. Now we hunt.'

'Just settle down,' he said mildly. He listened to the news reports with half an ear. The usual mayhem and gossip, but no frantic bulletins about man-eating demons on the loose in New York.

'Why are they here?' he asked her. 'Why leave one world for another?'

'Sorak is greedy, and his hunger is great. For flesh, but also for power. There are more of you in this place than on our world. And you are unaware. They can move among you without fear of the slayer. They will feed, gluttonously. First on animals, for quick strength, then on humans. Those that he and his warriors do not consume, he will change so he can build a vast army. They will overtake the world you know and make it theirs.'

'Whoa, back up. Change? What do you mean by change?'

'He will turn selected humans into demons, into slaves and warriors and concubines.'

'You're telling me he can make people into things? Like, what, vampires?'

'I do not know this word. Explain.'

'Never mind.' Harper pushed himself to his feet to pace. For reasons he couldn't explain, the idea of having human beings turned into monsters was more disturbing than having them served up as demon meals. 'How do they do it? How are people changed?'

'The Demon Kiss. Mouth against mouth. Tongue, teeth, lips. A bite, to draw blood, to mix it. Then the demon draws in the human essence, breathes his own into his prey. They are changed, and are compelled to hunt, to feed. They remember nothing of their humanity. This is worse than death.'

'Yeah.' The thought sickened him. 'Yeah, it's worse. No way this son of a bitch is going to turn my town into his personal breeding ground.' When he faced her, his face was set, and the warrior gleam in his eye gave Kadra her first real hope. 'Animals, you said. Cats, dogs, what?'

'These are pets.' She closed her eyes and searched the knowledge. 'Such small prey would not please them. This would do only if the hunger was impossible. They prefer the flesh of the unicorn above all.'

'Unicorns don't spend a lot of time grazing in New York. Horses?'

'Yes, horses, cows, goats. But there are no farms, you said. In the wild, they feed often on the lion or the ape.'

'Lions, tigers, and bears? The zoo. We'll start there. As soon as we figure out how to outfit you so you blend in a little better with the general population.'

Frowning, she looked down at herself. 'I don't resemble the other females in your world?'

He scanned the breasts barely constrained by black leather, the long, lean torso, the swatch of leather over curvy hips. And those endless legs encased in boots. Not to mention a two-and-a-half-foot sword.

'I couldn't begin to tell you. Let's see what I can put together.'

When she came out of his bedroom fifteen minutes later, he decided she did more to sell a pair of Levi's than a million-dollar ad campaign. And the old denim shirt had never looked better.

'Baby, you are a picture.'

She studied herself in his mirror, and agreed. 'It is tolerable hunting gear.' Testing it, she executed several quick deep-knee bends that had Harper's blood pressure rising. 'It will do.' So saying, she picked up her sword.

'You can't walk around outside with that thing.'

She glanced up, smirked. 'So, do I slay demons with bad thoughts?'

'Aha, sarcasm. I like it. I've got something. Hold on.' He went to the closet, shoved through it and came out with a long black coat. 'A little warm for May, but we can't be picky.'

'Why do people in your world cover up so much flesh?'

'I ask myself that question every day.' He took another long look at her. Maybe, just maybe, if he'd been able to design his own ideal woman, he'd have come close to the reality of her. 'You going to wear the little crown?'

Her hand went to the gold on top of her head. 'This is the circle of my rank.'

'You want to blend in?' He lifted the circlet off, set it aside. 'Put on the coat and let's see.'

Scowling, she dragged the coat on, turned to him. 'You're

still going to turn heads and star in a lot of male fantasies tonight, but you'll do.'

Satisfied, he pulled on a battered bomber jacket, hitched it over his gun.

'I want one.'

He noted her look at his Glock. 'Yeah, I know. But I don't have one to spare.' He slid on sunglasses, grabbed his keys. 'Let's go.'

'Why do you cover your eyes?'

'Styling, baby. I've got a pair for you in my car.' He stopped at the elevator, pushed the Down button. 'Try not to talk to anybody. If we have to have a conversation, let me handle it.'

She started to object, but the wall opened. 'A portal? Where does it lead?'

'It's an elevator. It goes up, it goes down. A kind of trans-portation.'

'A box,' she nodded as she stepped in with him. 'That moves.' Her grin spread when she felt the shift. 'This is clever. Your world is very interesting.'

The doors opened on three, and a woman and small boy got on.

'The elevator,' Kadra said politely. 'Goes up and goes down.'

The woman slid an arm around the boy and drew him close to her side.

'Didn't I tell you to keep quiet?' Harper hissed when they reached the lobby and the woman hustled her son away.

'I spoke with good manners, and made no threat to her or her young.'

'Just stick close,' he ordered, and took her hand firmly in his.

When they stepped outside, he thought it was a good thing he had a grip on her. She froze in place, her head swiveling right and left. 'What a world this is,' she breathed. 'Blue sky, great huts, so many people. So many scents. There.' She pointed to a sidewalk vendor. 'This is food.'

'Later.' He pulled her along the sidewalk. 'My car's in a garage a couple blocks over.'

'The ground is made of stone.'

He had to jerk her up when she bent over to tap a fist on the sidewalk. 'Concrete. Men make it and pour it over the ground.'

'Why? Is the ground poisonous?'

'No. It's just easier.'

'How can it be easier? The ground was already there.' She stopped again, mouth agape as an ambulance whizzed by, sirens screaming, lights flashing. 'Is it a war?'

'No, it's transportation. For the sick or the wounded.'

She digested this and other wonders on the two-block hike. The shops with their goods locked behind glass, the crowds of people in a hurry, the clatter and din of the machines that ran on the wide stone road.

'This is a noisy world,' she commented. 'I like it. What are these trees?' she asked, knocking a fist on a telephone pole.

'I'll explain later. Just say nothing.'

Harper strolled into the garage with a death grip on Kadra's hand. He flipped a salute to the attendant, who was passing the time with a magazine. But one look at Kadra had the attendant gaping.

'Oooh, baby! That *is fine.*'

'Why am I called baby here?' she demanded as he whipped into the stairway. 'I am not new young.'

'It's an expression. Endearment or insult, depending on your point of view.' On the second level, he crossed the lines of cars and stopped at his beloved '68 Mustang. He unlocked it, opened the passenger door. 'Climb in.'

She sniffed first, caught the scent of leather and approved. She was already fiddling with dials and jiggling the gearshift when he got behind the wheel. 'Don't touch.' He slapped her hand away. She kicked her elbow under his jaw. 'Cut it out.' Shoving her arm down, he reached for her seat belt. 'You need to strap in. It's the law of the land.'

When he bent to buckle her up, he saw that she was still miffed. 'You sure push my buttons,' he muttered.

'This is an expression?'

'Yeah. It means—'

'I do not need an explanation. You are aroused by me.'

'And then some.' He trailed his fingers over her cheek. Then he opened the glove compartment and tossed a pair of wraparound shades in her lap. 'I guess we have to go kick some demon butt before we deal with our buttons.'

4

She had a great deal to think about.

She was primarily a physical creature. When she was hungry, she ate. When she was tired, she slept. And all of her life, her purpose, above all others, had been to hunt.

It was a sacred trust, a sacred gift. She could laugh and weep, desire and dislike, dream and act. But over it all, through every cell in her body was the purpose.

She had been born, raised and trained for it.

But no slayer lived long if she didn't use her brain as well as her might.

Even with the wonder of her first car ride, the thrill of seeing the structures and the people, hearing the blasts of horns, of music, of voices, her mind still chipped away at the puzzle.

She had been sent to this place, and to this man. So their destinies were joined. She would protect him and his people with her life.

He was a seeker, and deserved respect. But as a slayer she ranked highest, save for the sorcerer. And if Rhee had spoken true, she had that in her blood as well.

The man had no right to usurp her authority. He would have to be put in his place for it.

But he was correct. This was his world, and his knowledge of it exceeded hers. If he was to be her guide, then she must follow. However much it rankled.

She desired him, which both pleased and irritated her. Pleased because he was strong and handsome, amusing and intelligent – and he desired her in turn. Irritated because she was unused to experiencing a desire this keen without the time and means to act upon it.

And she was not prepared for what was tangled in and woven through that desire. Lust was appetite, which could be easily sated. But this longing fluttering inside her, like a wild bird fighting to be free, was stronger, stranger than any need of the flesh.

65

It distracted her, and she could not afford to be distracted. If the Bok escaped her, this world, and her world, were doomed.

'So, how'd you get into the slayer business?'

She turned her head, and even with the dark glasses, Harper felt the heat of her gaze. 'It was a gift, given me at my creation. It is woven in my blood, in my bone.'

'Let's put it this way. You didn't pop out of the womb with a broadsword in your hand and a little dagger clenched in your teeth.'

'I was trained.' She liked watching the lights turn colors. She'd processed their purpose herself because she was tired of asking questions. 'To track, to hunt, in weaponry. To fight, to build my body, my mind, my spirit.'

'How about your parents?'

'I know no father. It is the way of slayers.'

'All slayers are women?'

'We are female, birthed by females, raised, trained, and tested.'

'What do the guys do? The men.'

'Males hunt, farm, become warriors, scholars, seekers like yourself.' She shrugged. 'Whatever path is open to them. Some, in protecting their land, their families, in battle or in defense of self, kill demons. But they are not slayers.'

'Are there more like you back home?'

'There were ten, now there are nine. Four weeks past, Sorak killed one of us. A trap. He drank the blood of a slayer. That is how he had the power, the strength, to elude me, to get this far. She was Laris. She was my friend.'

'I'm sorry.' Harper closed a hand over hers. 'He'll pay for it.'

The gesture, the simple warmth and connection, moved her. 'There is no payment rich enough. His death will have to do.' She looked over quickly when he lifted her hand to his mouth, brushed his lips over her knuckles.

'A custom,' he said, reading her shock. 'Like an expression. Comfort, affection, seduction. Whatever fits.'

Her lips curved. 'In my world you would be thrashed for taking such a liberty with a slayer.'

'We're in my world now, baby.'

'And here the sky is different, and the ground. The customs. I enjoy many of the new things in this place. The drink called coffee, the elevator, and the car. I have not decided if I like the box called television or all your expressions, but I enjoy the sensation of your mouth on my skin.'

He parked the car, turned off the ignition. 'You got a man back home? A lover?'

'No.'

'You're going to have one here.' He climbed out, skirted the hood, and opened her door. 'We'll walk for a while,' he told her and took her hand again. 'Stay close.'

She let him lead. It gave her the opportunity to observe and absorb, to identify scents. Food came to her again – sweet, spiced, tart. Her stomach tightened in hunger. Perhaps traveling through the portal sharpened the appetites, she thought. If that were true for the Bok, they would already have fed at least once.

She caught the scent of animal among the human. Great cats, reptile, fowl, and more she couldn't identify. And then she saw them, exotic beasts, prowling or dozing in enclosures while people strolled past or stopped to stare.

It gave her a pang at the most elemental level. 'It is not right to lock them up. They are not born for this.'

'Maybe it's not,' he agreed. He hadn't come to the zoo since childhood because it invariably made him sad. 'I can't say I care for it either.'

'This is a cruel thing you do here. This is a sorry place, this zoo. Is this what you teach your young?' she demanded, gesturing to a little girl being wheeled in a stroller by her parents. 'That one species can be locked away for the amusement of another?'

'I don't know how to explain it to you. Civilization has

encroached. There isn't as much room as there once was. In captivity, they're safe, I guess, and tended. They can't be hunted or taken as trophies.'

'They are not free,' was all she said, and turned away.

'Okay, maybe this was a bad idea. It's depressing, and the place is jammed. I wasn't thinking about it being Sunday. It doesn't seem like the time and place for a demon snack. Maybe we should try the animal shelter – dogs and cats. Or hit the stables.'

She held up a hand, bared her teeth. 'Bok,' was all she said.

She was on the scent and ran like the wind. People scrambled out of her way, and those who caught a glimpse of the sword under her coat scrambled faster and farther.

It was a challenge to keep up with her under normal circumstances, but with the obstacle course of people, children, benches, and trash receptacles in the zoo, Harper's lungs were burning by the time he caught up.

'Slow down,' he snapped. 'You mow down innocent bystanders, we'll get arrested before we get where you want to go. And I can't begin to tell you how much fun the cops will have with your demon story.'

'There!' She pointed to a building, seconds before a stream of people rushed out. Screaming.

She drew her sword as she raced through the doorway.

Whatever Harper had expected, it hadn't been this, this stench of blood and death, of fear and rot. In the cages, monkeys were wild. Screeching, screaming, leaping desperately from branch to branch.

He saw the blood and gore on the floor, tracked it with his eyes, and found – to his horror – a man, no, a demon, feeding savagely on a body. A human body.

When the demon lifted his head, his teeth, his eyes glistened red.

It all happened in seconds. The shock, the disgust, the fury. All of those vicious sensations burst through him as Harper drew his gun. And something hideous pounced on his back.

Claws dug into his shoulders, gouged as the thing that attacked him let out a predatory howl. He spun, ramming back into the wall. His gun flew out of his hand and slid across the floor. Cursing, he battered the thing against the wall as his own blood spilled hot down his back. He felt the rough edge of a tongue slide through it, slurp hideously.

Revolted, he flew back with his elbow, aiming high for the throat, hammered down with his heel on the instep of a booted foot hard enough to hear bone snap.

There was a shriek, inhuman. Harper jabbed behind him with his fingers where he hoped to find eyes.

Now it screamed, and the claws released.

He saw what it was now, as he spun around. The face of a man, the eyes of a monster. It came for him, and Harper sprang into the fight.

It was limping from the bones he'd crushed, but it was still fast. Lightning fast. Harper whirled, and the thing hurtled past him. When it turned to charge again, he met its face with a flying kick.

Kadra fought her own demons, swinging her sword to block the slice of a curved blade, evading the swipe of claws as she carefully retreated. She gauged Harper's position by sound. She couldn't risk even a glance behind her. Out of the corner of her eye, she saw Sorak, behind the bars, grinning, grinning as he feasted and watched the battle.

Kadra flipped her dagger out of its sheath, managed to turn enough to judge Harper's distance and position. She feinted, thrust, then leaped to cleave the demon's sword arm from his body.

'Harper Doyle!' She shouted, then heaved him her sword as she snatched the sickle blade from the air to battle the next demon.

They fought back-to-back now, Harper wielding the

sword, she slicing with the dagger and blade. Green blood mixed with red.

Still, she saw, Sorak watched.

'I will have you,' he called out. 'I will have your blood. I will have your body. I will have your mind.'

'I am Kadra!' she almost sang it as she thrust through slicing claws and pinned the point of the dagger in the demon warrior's throat. 'I am your death.' She spun, prepared to leap into the other battle. And watched Harper's sword cleave his opponent's belly.

Through the smoke curling from the demon dead, she scooped the Glock up on the fly as she rushed to where Sorak fed and gloated. She saw only the quick flash of his teeth, the taunting swirl of his cloak as he bolted toward an open door on the side of the cage.

She fired, the explosions of sound roaring through the building. Even so, she could hear the demon's laughter. She vaulted over the safety rail, closed her hands on the bars of the cage where beasts lay slaughtered, and battered at the steel.

'Come on.' Riding on adrenaline and pain, Harper wrenched her around. He shot the sword back into her sheath, snatched his gun and holstered it. 'Put this away. Now,' he snapped, handing her the dagger. 'We're getting out, fast. There's no possible explanation for what just happened here, so we're not going to make one. Move!'

She ran with him, through the building, out the rear. He tugged the coat over her sword, wrapped an arm around her shoulders, and tried to look as normal as a couple could who had just battled a pack of demons.

'Keep it slow. Cops are already heading in.' He heard the sirens, the shouts. They turned away from the noise and kept walking. How long had they been inside? he wondered. It had seemed like hours. But now he realized it had been only minutes.

'Can you track it?' Harper asked her.

Alone, on her world, the answer would have been yes. But here, with the crowds of people, the scents and sights so unfamiliar to her senses, she was unsure.

'He will go to ground now. He knew. He knew I would come here. Sorak has more knowledge than I thought. Now he has fed, he has amused himself. He will rest and wait. He will not feed again in the daylight.'

'Just as well. The place is going to be crawling with cops. Since we're covered with blood, and armed, we wouldn't get very far.'

And he had a bad feeling that a lot of the blood was his own. He wouldn't be any good to Kadra in the next round if he was light-headed and shocky. First things first, he thought as he concentrated on staying upright. Get bandaged up, get steady. Then think.

'We'll hunt the bastard down and kill him with his belly full.'

It was difficult to turn away from the hunt. But she had seen the demon attack him from the rear and knew he was wounded. She would not leave him behind.

'He has disguised his scent with the animals, and the humans. He will take time for me to find his lair.' She steadied him when he swayed against her, and the hand she pressed to his shoulder came away smeared with his blood.

'How bad is your wound?'

'I don't know. Bad enough. Fucking claws. Went right through the leather. I've only had this jacket five, six years.'

She turned her head to look at the gouges and was relieved to see the demon had torn more cloth than flesh. 'It is not so bad. It was a good battle,' she said with sudden cheer. 'You fight well.'

'Three out of four. It's just the one now.'

'He will make more.'

The horror of that seized Harper's belly. 'We have to stop him.'

'We will do what must be done. Now we go back to

your hut. Your wounds must be tended. We will rest, eat, think. We will be ready for the night.'

Her unerring sense of direction took them back to his car. 'Can I sit on the side with the wheel now?'

'No, you can't sit on the side with the wheel now. Or ever.' Hurting, exhausted, he jabbed the key into the lock, wrenched open the door.

'Are all so selfish with their possessions here?'

'A man's car is his castle,' Harper stated, and limped around to take the wheel. 'Are you hurt?' he remembered to ask.

'No, I am unharmed.' Realizing he might take this as a criticism of his skill, she took his hand as he had taken hers. 'But I am a slayer.'

'Kiss ass.'

She cocked her head. The battle had lifted her mood. 'This is another expression?'

He had to laugh, had to hiss in pain. On a combination of both, he started the car. 'Yeah, baby, but it's one I wouldn't mind you taking literally.'

5

Though sheer will kept Harper conscious, he was in considerable pain and woozy from the loss of blood by the time he pulled back into his slot at the garage. Kadra's idea of how to deal with the problem was to carry him.

He had just enough strength left to stop her from slinging him over her shoulder. And just enough wit to realize she could have pulled it off.

'No.' Since his limbs had gone watery on him, he warded her off with a scowl. 'I'm not being carried across the Lower East Side by a woman.'

'This is foolish. You're injured. I am not.'

'Yeah, yeah, keep rubbing it in. Just give me a hand.'

When she frowned and held one out, he shook his head. 'You're a literal creature.' He slid an arm around her waist, let her take some of his weight. 'Walk and talk,' he told her. 'Tell me more about this change.'

'After the kiss of change, the victim falls into a trance — a sleep that is not a sleep, for one day. During the sleep, the demon blood mixes with the human's. The human becomes what has poisoned him, with the demon's instincts, his habits. His appetites.'

Since Harper's breathing was ragged, she tightened her grip and shortened her stride. 'When the human wakes he is demon, though some wake before the change is complete and are demi-demons. In either stage, the one who has changed is bound to the one who changed him.'

'Is there a cure?'

'Death,' she said flatly, and shifted her grip on him as they stepped outside. He was pale, she noted. And his breath was only more labored. It would have been easier to carry him.

But she understood a warrior's pride.

'Your hut is only a short journey. We will go at your pace.'

'Just keep talking.' His shoulder was going numb, and that worried him. 'I need to focus.'

'Why did you become a seeker?'

'I like to find things out. Without a PI license, it's called nosiness. With one, it's called a profession. Insurance fraud, missing persons, some skip tracing. I try to stay out of the marital arena. It's just humiliating for all parties to stand outside a motel room with a camera.'

She didn't know what he was talking about, but she liked his voice. Despite his wounds, or perhaps because of them, there was grit in it. 'Are you a successful seeker?'

'I get by.' He looked around but couldn't quite pinpoint where they were. The sounds of traffic, the busy music of the city, sounded dim. She was the only thing clear to him now – the supporting strength of her arm, the firm curves of her body, the scent of the sacred waterfall that lingered in her hair.

It was as if both their worlds had receded and they themselves were all that was left.

'What must you get by?'

'Hmm?' He turned his head. He'd been right, he thought, there really was nothing but her. 'I mean I do all right. I do regular legwork for a lawyer. Jake, the one I thought had hired you. He's got a sick sense of humor. That's why I love him.'

He staggered at the curb, tried to orient himself when she

steadied him. 'It is this way.' She turned the corner, glanced up and down the street. 'Where is the well? You require water.'

'Doesn't work that way here.' But she was right about one thing. His thirst was vicious. He nodded toward a sidewalk vendor. 'There.'

With her arm banded around his waist, Kadra watched Harper exchange several small disks for a bottle. He fought the top off, drank deep.

'You must pay for water? Does it have magical properties?' She took it, drank. 'Nothing but water,' she said with some amazement. 'The merchant is a robber. I will go back and speak to him.'

'No. No.' Despite the dizziness, Harper laughed. 'It's just one of the acceptable lunacies of our little world. When water comes out of the tap, it's free. Sort of. When it comes out of a bottle, you pay on the spot.'

She pondered this as they came to the intersection. She'd watched the way the people, the cars, the lights worked together. When the metal tree ordered the waiting group to walk, everyone hurried, often sliding and swooping between cars that jammed together and faced other metal trees with lights of amber, emerald, and ruby.

Everyone in the village played along.

She felt Harper sag, and pinched his waist ruthlessly to snap him back. 'We have only . . . ' She flipped back to his earlier term for the section of road. 'One more block.'

'Okay, okay.' He could feel sweat running a clammy line down his back. His vision was going in and out. 'Let's talk about me. I'm thirty. As of yesterday. Unmarried. Came close a couple years ago, but I came to my senses.'

'Had the woman bewitched you?'

'No.' He had to smile at the term. 'You could say that was the problem: she *didn't* bewitch me. This is a huge disappointment to my parents, who want grandchildren. As I'm an only child, I'm their one shot at it.'

'Is it not possible in this place to make young without a lifemate? Can you not select a breeding partner for this purpose?'

'Yeah, you could, and a lot of people do. I guess I'm more of a traditionalist in that one area. If I have kids, I want them to have the package. You like kids?'

'I am fond of young. They have innocence and potential, and a special kind of beauty. In time I will select a breeding partner so that I may make life. It is a great honor to make life.'

'I'm with you on that.' Nearly there, he told himself. Please, God, we're nearly there. 'Anyway, my parents live in New Jersey. Another world.'

'Was Old Jersey destroyed?'

'Ah . . . no.' His head was spinning now. Concentrate, he ordered himself. Just put one foot in front of the other. 'Geography and world history lessons later. Let's stick with personal revelations. I didn't want to tie on my dad's cop's shoes, so I veered off into private investigation. I apprenticed with a big, slick firm uptown, but I didn't like the suit-and-tie brigade. Went out on my own about five years ago. I'm good at what I do.'

'It's wasteful to be bad at what you do.'

'You know, my dad would lap you right up. He'd like you,' Harper explained, breathlessly now. 'He was a good cop. Retired three years ago. He'd go for your sense of order.'

He fumbled out his keys as they approached his building's entrance. She wanted to ask him why everything had to be locked, like a treasure box, but his face was dead white now.

She dragged him to the elevator, puzzled out the buttons. They had come down, so now they would go up. It pleased her enormously when the doors opened.

'Four,' he managed. 'Push four. If we have to call 911, I'm going to leave it to you to explain that I've been clawed by a Bok demon.'

Ignoring him, and regretting that she couldn't fully

appreciate the ride this time, she dragged him out when the doors opened again. She took the keys from him, selected the proper one, and unlocked his door.

'You don't miss a trick, do you? You'd make a damn good PI.'

She merely booted the door closed behind them, then bending, lifted him onto her shoulder.

'Honey.' His voice slurred. 'This is so sudden.'

She laid him facedown on the bed, peeled off his ruined jacket, then tore away what was left of his shirt.

His breath hissed through his teeth at the bright burn of pain. 'Can you be a little more rough, Nurse Ratched? I live for pain.'

'Quiet now.' The wounds were deeper than she'd thought. Four ugly grooves and one jagged puncture. The blood that had started to clot flowed freely again. 'This must first be cleansed. How do I fetch water?'

'Tap. Bathroom tap. The sink. Damn it. The white bowl – ah, the taller one,' he added as he got an image of her scooping water out of his toilet. 'Turn the handle.'

She found the bathing room, and the sink. And was delighted when water gushed out. She soaked a towel and carried it sopping wet into the bedroom. She felt his body shudder when she laid it over his back.

He fought well, she thought again as she cleaned the wounds. And was stalwart in his pain. He had more than the strength of a warrior; he had the heart of one too. She remembered how his hand had whipped up and closed around the hilt of the sword she'd tossed him.

A good team, she decided. She'd never found a partner she could admire, respect, and desire.

She retrieved her supply bag, reached in for the vial of healing powder that all warriors carried. Her fingers brushed over the cloth Mav had wrapped around her hand.

Lips pursed, Kadra studied her own unmarked palm. Perhaps some of the healer's powers were still in the cloth. Quickly, she made a paste from powder and water.

'This will sting,' she told him. 'I'm sorry for it.'

'Sting' was a mild word for the blaze that erupted under his skin when she spread the medication over his wounds. His hands fisted in the spread, his body jerked in protest.

'Only a moment,' she murmured, wrenched by his pain. 'It eats any infection.'

'Does it chew through flesh while it's at it?' He spit the words out through gritted teeth.

'No, but it feels that way. It is no shame to scream.'

'I'll keep that in mind.' But he swore instead, softly, steadily, viciously, and earned more of the slayer's respect.

When the paste began to turn from sickly yellow to white, she breathed a sigh of relief. The infection was dying. Over the smeared wounds, she lay the thin healing cloth.

'If there is any magic in my blood,' she whispered, 'let it help him. Sleep now, Harper the valiant.' She brushed her fingers through his hair. 'Sleep and heal.'

He dreamed, strange, colorful dreams. Battles and blood. Storms and swords. Kadra, with her war cry echoing through dark, dank tunnels. The king of demons feasting on flesh in the shadows.

And he himself delivering the killing blow that sent green blood gushing.

In dreams he knew her body, the feel of those luscious curves under his hand, the taste of her skin, the sound of her moan. He saw her rising over him, warrior, goddess, woman.

He felt, real as life, the warm press of her lips on his.

And woke aching for her.

He sat up, instinctively reaching for the back of his shoulder. He found nothing, no wound, no break in the skin, no scar.

Had it all been a dream after all? One wild booze-induced dream starring the most magnificent woman ever created?

The idea that she was only in his mind depressed him brutally. What were a few Bok demons between friends, he thought as he pushed himself out of bed, when you had a Kadra in your life?

Was the only woman who'd ever stirred him on every level just a product of his imagination? Of wishful thinking? If he could only fall in love in dreams, why the hell did he have to wake up?

Back to reality, Doyle, he told himself, then took a step toward the bedroom door and nearly tripped over his leather jacket.

He scooped it up, fingers rushing over the battered material. Nothing, nothing in his life had ever delighted him more than seeing those bloodstained rips.

He tossed it aside and bolted for the door.

She'd changed back into her own clothes. And was sitting cross-legged on the floor, her nose all but pressed to the television screen, where the Yankees were taking on the Tigers.

'I like this battle,' she said without turning around. 'The warriors in the white are beating the warriors in the gray by three runs. They are better with the clubs.'

'Girl of my dreams,' Harper said aloud. 'She likes baseball.'

'There were other images in the box.' And each had startled and fascinated. 'But this is my favorite.'

'Okay, that does it. We have to get married.'

She turned then, smiled at him. His color was back, and that relieved her. His eyes were clear, and held more than recovered health. The lust in them aroused her. 'You healed well.'

'I healed just dandy.'

'I hunted among your stores,' she told him. 'You have little, but I like this food and drink.' She gestured toward the bag of sour-cream-and-onion potato chips and the bottle of Coors.

'You're perfect. It's just a little scary.'

'We must eat. Fighting requires fuel.'

'Yeah, we'll eat. We'll order some pizza.'

He looked hungry as well, she noted. But not for food. She rose smoothly. Her blood was already warm for him. 'I'm pleased you are well.'

'Yeah. I'm feeling real healthy just now. You can tell me how you managed that later.'

'You do not wish to talk at this time.' She nodded, stepped toward him. Then she circled around him to check his shoulder – and to admire his form. When she stopped face-to-face again, her eyes were level with his. 'Do you wish to join your body to mine?'

He blinked once, slow as an owl. 'Is that a trick question?'

'You have desire for me.'

Charmed, perplexed, he dipped his hands in his pockets. 'Is that all it takes?'

'No.' She was never as sure of herself as a female as she was as a slayer. But this time, with him, she felt sure. 'But I have desire for you as well. It is a heat in my belly, a burn in my blood. I want to join with you.'

'I wanted you before I even met you,' he told her.

'This is like a poem.' And softened her under the skin. 'You are well named. I cannot speak as cleverly, so I will say we have time for this and for food before we hunt again. And that our minds and bodies will be stronger for appeasing both appetites.'

On those long, tantalizing legs, she walked past him into the bedroom.

Worlds, he thought as he followed her, were about to collide.

'Whoa. Wait. Hold on.' She'd already stripped off her top, and was pulling off her boots. 'What's the rush?'

She looked up, a crease between her brows. 'Are you ready to sport?'

'Yeah. But we could take a minute to . . . ' He stared at her, golden skin, naked breasts. 'What am I saying?' He scooped her off her feet and made her laugh by tossing her on the bed.

She rolled, came up on her haunches. Saliva pooled in his mouth as she grinned at him. 'You have energy. Good. Strip,' she ordered. 'We will wrestle first.'

'You wanna wrestle?' He unbuttoned his jeans.

'It is stimulating,' she began, then lowered her gaze. 'You seem to be very stimulated already. I admire your body, baby.' It pleased her to use one of his terms of affection. 'I want to touch it.'

'Are you sure you're not a dream, brought on by one too many bourbons and bumps?'

'I am real.' Watching him, she stroked her hands over her breasts, cupped them. 'Touch me.'

When he came forward, reached, she rolled away laughing. And crooked her finger at him.

He dived.

She obviously took her wrestling seriously – he was pinned in under five seconds. 'Two out of three,' he said and put himself in the game.

They tumbled over the bed, hands gripping, sliding, legs scissoring. Bodies straining. He wasn't sure if he pinned her by skill or because she'd allowed it. He didn't give a damn. Not when she was sprawled under him, her hair spread out, her eyes hot and green.

'Let's call it a draw,' he suggested, lowering his head.

Her hand shot out, wedged between them. 'There can be no mouth on mouth. This is not permitted.'

'Kisses are illegal in your world?'

'A kiss is a gift.' Now it was she who was breathless, from the press of his body, from the knowledge that his lips were nearly upon hers. 'One given in promise between those who mate.'

'I had mating in mind.'

'No, joining. Joining is . . . sport. Mating is for life.'

He wanted that mouth, as much as he wanted to breathe. And he wanted her to give it to him. 'In this world a kiss is a sign of trust, affection, love, friendship. All manner of things. When a man and a woman join here, a kiss is a part of the union. A pleasurable part. You've never kissed a man?'

'I've made no promise to a man with my lips.'

Make one to me, he thought. 'Let me show you the way it's done in my world.' He brushed his lips over her cheek. 'Let me have your mouth, Kadra.'

The hand separating them began to tremble. 'I can take no lifemate.' She felt his breath on her lips, warm, seductive. 'It is not permitted for a slayer in my world.'

'This is here. This is now.' He closed his hand over the one she still held to his heart. 'Let me be the first. Let me be the only.'

She could have resisted. She had the strength, and though

she could feel it melting, she still had the will. But his lips were so lovely, so soft against her skin. The glide of them was like all the promises that could never be given.

And her own lips yearned.

His world, she thought as she yielded. She was in his world now.

Their lips met, silkily. And her breath rushed out in shock at the sensation. The intimacy, the sweet flavor, the smooth slide of tongue against tongue were more potent than any brew she had ever sipped.

With one drink, she was drunk on him.

'Again,' she demanded, and dragged him down by the hair until mouth ravaged mouth.

He had thought a kiss a simple thing, just another part of the mating dance. But with her he was whirled into the glory of it. He sank deep into her, and deeper still, until the taste of her was a craving in his belly.

I've waited for you, she thought, bowing her body to his − a body that ached for his hands. How could I have waited for you when I didn't know you existed? How could I have needed you when you were never there?

But when his hands moved over her, she knew it was true. All the passion that was in her blood, all the passion newly discovered, she gave to him.

She was a fantasy come to life. All curves and sleek skin. Urgent hands and avid mouth. She raged beneath him, demanding more even as he gave. She was a feast who commanded him to feed.

Now when they wrestled, their breath was ragged and their skin damp. The mouth that had conquered hers rushed everywhere, tasted all of her.

When she crested, it was like a wave rising up inside her, spilling out on a throaty cry and pouring into him.

She rose above him, as she had in dreams. Woman, warrior, lover. She took him into her, closed around him, and throwing her head back, rode.

Joined, he thought dimly as his blood pounded. Everything inside him was joined with her.

He reared up, banding his arms around her, fusing his mouth to hers as they took each other over the brink.

6

No joining had ever been so intense or so pleasurable. None had caused her to feel this mysterious sensation that was beyond the physical. Nor to find herself both conquered and victorious.

Bards spoke of such unions, but she had never believed the words were more than romantic delusion.

And they were joined still, she realized. Wrapped tight, fused like two links in one chain. This was more than sport, she thought. She didn't wish it to end.

She rubbed her lips together, experimenting. His taste was still there – his flesh, yes – but it was more. His mouth, the intimacy of the kiss that had been like . . . feeding each other. She hadn't known such matters could have such heat, and yet be tender.

She had never known tenderness, nor had she believed she required it.

Small wonder that in the world she knew, a mouth kiss was reserved for lifemates and was part of the sacred vows that stretched for all time.

If he lived in her world, or she in his, could there have been a lifetime between them?

Thinking it brought such a pang, such a wrench of longing. She was a slayer, she reminded herself, and he a seeker. They could walk the same path only until their battle was won. Then they, like their worlds, would stand apart.

But until their time was ended, she could have what she could take.

'I like the kissing,' she said, sliding her hands into his hair as she eased back to see his face. 'I would like to do more if there's an opportunity to join again.'

'Kissing isn't just for joining.' Still lost in her, still steeped in the first heady brew of love, he brushed his lips across hers.

'What else? Teach me.'

At the idea of tutoring her, his pulse kicked again. 'At times like this, after making love—'

'Making love.' Following his lead, she leaned in to rub her lips over his. 'I like this expression.'

'Sometimes, after, while a couple is still tuned to each other, they kiss to show how much pleasure they were given. It might be long and lazy, like this.'

He drew her in again on a slow, gentle glide that brought a purr of approval to her throat. Soft, so soft, deep without demand. Sweet as a maiden's dream.

'Yes,' she sighed. 'Again.'

'Wait. Sometimes, when passions have been roused and people are still caught in that last edge of the storm of them, the tone of the kiss reflects that. Like this.'

He caught her to him, close and hard, and his mouth was like a fever on hers. Now she groaned and wrapped around him like rope. He felt the thrill of her on his skin, in his blood, down to the pit of his stomach.

'You make me want.' Her voice was thick now, and her heart galloped as if she'd raced to the pinnacle of the Stone Mountains. 'In ways I have never wanted.'

'You make me need.' He held her now, just held her. 'In ways I've never needed. What are we going to do about this, Kadra?'

She shook her head. 'What must be done is all that can be done.'

'Things have changed. Things are different now.'

If only they could be, she thought. With him, a joy she hadn't known was locked inside her could be free. 'What I feel for you fills me, and empties me. I've never known this with another.' Still, she made herself draw back from him. 'The fate of two worlds is in our hands. We can't take each other and lose them.'

'We'll save them. And then—'

'Don't talk of "and then."' She touched her fingers to his lips. 'Whatever fate holds for us, we have now. It's a gift to be treasured, not to be questioned.'

'I want a life with you.'

She smiled, but there was sorrow in her eyes. 'Some lifetimes have to be lived in a day.'

He wasn't going to accept that. He was good at solving puzzles, Harper thought. He'd find a way to solve this one. He also knew when he was banging against a head as hard as his own. There were times for force, and times for strategy.

'Having a warrior goddess drop on me out of another dimension, visiting an alternate reality, fighting demons, making love. It's been a pretty full day so far.' He tangled his fingers in her hair. 'What's next on the schedule?'

Strength, Kadra thought, wasn't only a matter of muscle. It was a matter of courage. They would both be valiant enough to accept destiny. 'We must hunt Sorak, but we will need food and planning time. He's the mightiest of his kind, and the most sly.'

'Okay, we'll order that pizza and fuel up while we figure out our plan of attack.'

Nodding, and grateful he hadn't pressed where she was now vulnerable, she rolled off the bed. 'What is this pizza?'

No pizza on A'Dair, he thought. Score one for Earth. 'It's, ah, a kind of pie. Round, usually,' he said as he allowed himself the pleasure of watching her slip on the brief bottom half of her hunting costume.

'You're magnificent, Kadra. "Beautiful" is too ordinary, too simple a word,' he added when she stared at him. 'Do men on A'Dair tell you that you take their breath away, that looking at you is like being struck blind by a force of beauty so strong it's painful?'

His words made her weak, as if she'd slain a thousand demons in one day. 'Men do not speak so to slayers.'

He rose. 'I do.'

'You are different.' So wonderfully different. 'When I hear the words from you, they make me feel proud. And shy.

I have never been shy,' she added, baffled. 'It pleases me that you find me attractive to look at.'

'Do you think that's all I meant? You are very attractive. You're right off the charts in that area. But then you add the courage, the brains, the compassion I saw in you when Mav told you of her father's death, the active curiosity, the sense of fun, the heart of a warrior. You're unique to any world, and I'm dazzled by you.'

'No one has ever . . .' Her throat burned. 'I need time to find the words to give back to you that are as fine and rich.'

He took her hands, lifted them to his lips. 'They were free. They don't require any trade or payment.'

'Like a gift?'

'Exactly.'

'Thank you.'

He dressed, switched the TV to the news in case there were any updates. He started to call in the pizza order. Then he remembered it wasn't just his taste that had to be satisfied this time. 'Okay, pizza can come with a variety of options. Meat, vegetables – stuff like onions, mushrooms, peppers, sausage, pepperoni. It's an endless parade. I usually get it pretty loaded. Is there anything you don't eat?'

'I don't care for the meat of the grubhog.'

He let out a quick, huffing laugh. 'Check. Hold the grub-hog.'

He called in the order – explained to her what a phone was – then went into the kitchen for a couple of beers. 'It'll take about twenty minutes. Let's figure out what step we take next over a beer.'

'I like the beer,' she told him.

'Just one more reason we're perfect for each other.' He tapped his bottle to hers. 'So.' He dropped down on the couch, stretched out. 'You said Sorak would have a lair. What sort of digs would he look for? What's his habit in living arrangements?'

'Demons live belowground.' She crossed her feet at the ankles, then lowered herself in one smooth move to the floor. 'They like the dark after feeding. They will burrow, dig tunnels so they may travel under the ground.'

She picked up the portable phone he'd set down and began to play with it.

'In the east, Laris and I once tracked a demon pack to a great lair, with many tunnels through the rock and dirt, with many chambers for stores and sleep and treasures. We slew the pack and destroyed the lair with fire. It was Clud's palace, and there I destroyed the king of demons. But Sorak, then prince, was not there. When he heard of this, he vowed to kill the

slayers who had killed his sire, and to build a great new kingdom in a place where no slayer could defeat him. I have this.'

She flipped back her hair to show him a thin hooked scar
at the base of her neck. 'Only a demon king can leave his
mark on a slayer. This is Clud's. The last swipe of his claws
before my sword took his heart.'

'Impressive.' Harper pulled down his shirt to expose the
line of puckered skin on his shoulder. 'Skip trace, with a bad
attitude and a switchblade.'

She nodded. 'How did you kill him?'

'It doesn't work that way here – ideally. I kicked his ass,
then turned him over to the cops and collected my fee. The
authorities,' he explained. 'We put bad guys – our demons –
in jail. In cages, like at the zoo today.'

'Ah.' She considered that, and found it just. Captivity was
a living death. 'Is the demon who broke your nose also in
his cage?'

'Sucker punch,' Harper told her, running his hand down
the uneven line of his nose. 'Yeah, he's doing a stretch.
Pissant grifter going around snuggling up to rich women,
then ripping them off, copping their jewelry, draining their
bank accounts. Prick.'

Kadra angled her head. 'I like the way you speak. I find
it arousing to listen to your stories.'

'Oh, yeah?' He slid down onto the floor beside her, walked his fingers up her boot to her thigh. 'I've got a million of them.'

'Sporting must wait.'

'I like your face. I find it arousing to look at your face.' He touched it, just a skim of fingertips over her cheek. 'When I was sleeping, I dreamed of making love with you. Then it happened, just the way I'd dreamed it.'

'This is vision.'

'Maybe.' He thought of the blood and the battle, of the dark and the smoke. 'One thing, before we get back on track. I've always liked working alone; that's why I went out on my own. I've liked living alone, which is why I've screwed up any potentially serious relationship with a woman. I never wanted a partner, until you.'

She lifted a hand to his cheek in turn. A kind of joining, she realized, with only a touch. 'I have been alone. It is the way of slayers. I never wished it otherwise, until you. They will write songs about you in my world. The great warrior from beyond A'Dair.'

And when she listened to them by the fire, she thought, she would be alone again.

She let her hand drop away, then took a deep drink of her beer. 'I tracked Sorak across my world and killed many of his warriors. He has sired no young, and with his death, the power of the Bok will be diminished. I thought he meant to build a lair in some far-off place, a fortress of great defense. But in my world. I did not know he meant to come to this place, to build his kingdom in yours.'

'We won't give him the chance. You said he would burrow underground.'

'Yes. The Bok require the cool dark when they rest.'

'I've got an idea where he might've gone. The subway. We have a system of tunnels under the city, for transportation. The sewers are another option,' Harper considered, 'but I don't know why anyone, even a demon, would want to set up housekeeping in the sewers if he had any other choices. The trick will be pinpointing the right sector.'

'What creatures of your world travel this subway, this underground route?'

'The variety is endless. Just people, of all walks. It's a crowded city. It's another reasonably efficient and inexpensive way to get around it.'

He spent the next few minutes explaining the idea and basic workings of the subway system.

'This is clever. You have an innovative and interesting culture. I would like to have more time to study it.'

'Stick around, take all the time you want.' He rose when his buzzer sounded. He went to the intercom by the front door, verified the pizza delivery, and buzzed the entrance door open.

'You keep a servant in that small box?'

'No.' Amused when she came over to peer at it, he explained its function, then opened his door to the delivery boy's knock, paid him, and sent him on his way.

'Was that your servant?'

'No. I gave my servants this century off. He works for the place that makes the food. It's his job to bring it to people when they call on the phone. Hungry?'

'Yes.' She sniffed. 'It smells very good.'

He set the pizza box on the coffee table. 'I'll get some napkins – we'll need them – then you can see if it tastes as good as it smells.'

When he came back she was sitting on the floor, the lid of the box open, poking a finger at the crust. 'It is very colorful. Is this a staple of your people's diet?'

'It's a staple of mine.' He lifted a slice, flicked strings of cheese with his finger. 'You just pick it up with your hands and go for it.' He demonstrated with an enthusiastic bite.

Following suit, Kadra brought a slice to her lips. She bit through pepperoni, through pepper, through onion into cheese and spicy sauce, down to the thin, yeasty crust.

The sound she made, Harper thought, was very like one she'd made during sex.

'I like this pie called pizza,' she stated, and bit in again. 'It is good food,' she added, her mouth full.

'Baby, this is the perfect food.'

'It goes well with the beer. It's like a celebration to have kissing and joining, then pizza and beer.'

He knew it was ridiculous, but his heart simply melted. 'I'm crazy about you, Kadra. I'm a goddamn mental patient.'

'This is an expression?'

'It means I'm in love with you. I go thirty years without a scratch, and in less than a day I'm fatally wounded.'

'Don't speak of death, even as an expression. Not before battle.' She reached out, closed her hand tight over his. 'It is bad luck. When it is done . . . When it is done, Harper, we will talk more of feelings.'

'All right, we'll table it – if I have your word that when it's done you let me make my pitch.'

Baffled, she frowned at him over what was left of her first slice. 'Like in the battle of baseball?'

'Not exactly. That you'll let me tell you the way it could be for us.'

'When it is done, you will make your pitch. Now tell me more of the subway.'

'Hold on.' He switched his attention to the televised news bulletin.

The reporter spoke of the attack at the zoo, the murder of the guard and the mutilation of several animals. Witness reports were confused and conflicting, ranging from the claim of an attack by a dozen armed men to one by a pack of wild animals.

'They don't know what they're up against,' Harper said quietly as the newscaster reported that the police were investigating the incident and that the zoo would remain closed until further notice. 'They don't have a clue. I call them with the truth, I'm just another loony.'

'It is for us,' Kadra told him. 'Rhee has said that we would fight this battle together. He must be destroyed here or driven back where he belongs. There must be balance again.'

'Here.' Harper rolled his shoulder where the demon had dug its claws. 'We finish it here. New York style.'

Kadra pondered the images on the television, the moving paintings of the zoo. 'This subway. Does it go near the place where they keep the animals? Where we battled today?'

'There are possibilities.'

'Sorak would like a lair near prey. It will be dark soon,' she said with a long look at the sky through the window. 'Then we hunt.'

7

She balked at changing her hunting gear for jeans a second time, claiming they restricted her. He let it pass, figuring the long coat would cloak most of her . . . attributes.

The thing about New York, Harper thought, as they passed a guy with shoulder-length white hair, two nose rings, and a black leather jumpsuit, was there was always someone dressed weirder than you were.

He wore his ripped jacket, for sentimental reasons. And for the practical one that if he was going up against a demon again, there was no point to sacrificing another garment to the long blue claws.

He had his Glock in a shoulder holster, a backup .38 in an ankle holster, a combat knife sheathed at his back, and a switchblade in his left boot.

He'd have preferred an Uzi, but what he had on hand would have to do.

'I like my work,' he told Kadra. 'And I like to think it makes a difference to some of the people who come to me with problems.' He paused to take a good look at his neighborhood – his city – his world. 'But this heading out to save the planet stuff brings on a real high.'

'You were born for it.' When he glanced over at her, she shrugged. 'This is what I believe. We are born for a purpose. How we live, how we treat others who live with us forms our spirit and determines if we will fulfill that purpose or fail. We were meant to face this night together. Meant for it from the moment we were created.'

'I like that. And I'll take it one step further. We were meant for each other, too.'

Meant to love each other, she thought, and to live alone in two different worlds. Her life had been filled with sacrifices, but none would bring the sorrow of the one she had yet to make.

Harper led Kadra down into the station for the train heading uptown. She would have vaulted over the turnstile if he hadn't blocked her.

'You have to use a token, then you walk through.'

'These are very flimsy barricades,' she pointed out as she bumped through. 'Even a child could get over them.'

'Yeah, well, it's ... tradition.'

'Like a ritual,' she decided, satisfied. She heard the roar, felt the floor vibrate. 'The earth trembles.' She was prepared to drag him to safety when he grabbed her hand.

'It's just a train coming in.' Still holding her hand, he pulled her onto the platform, where she studied the other waiting passengers.

It was a huge cave, strongly lit. She had never seen so much life, so much motion and magic in one place. 'Your people have so many colors of skin. It's beautiful. You are blessed to have such richness of person, such variety.' When she glanced back at him, she saw he was smiling at her in an odd way. 'What is it?'

'Nothing.' He leaned toward her, and to her utter shock, kissed her mouth.

'We cannot join here,' she said in a hissing whisper. 'It is a private activity.'

'It wasn't that kind of a kiss. Remember, there are all kinds.'

'I thought you were pretending.'

'Is that a polite word for lying? On this side of the portal, people kiss all the time. Lovers, friends, relatives. Complete strangers.'

She snorted. 'Now I will say you are lying.'

'Locking lips is practically a global pastime. And this one'll get you: people pay a fee to sit in a big, darkened room as a group and watch other people's images on a screen – a larger version of the TV, where you saw baseball. One of the things those images often do is kiss.'

'I think you are a harper after all, because you tell fantastic tales with great ease and skill.'

'Nothing in those knowledge banks about movies?'

She frowned, but tipped her head and searched through. When her eyes widened, lit with delight, he knew she'd hit on it.

'Movies.' She tested the word. 'I would like to see one.'

'It's a date.' He heard the rumble of the approaching uptown train. They had another date to keep first.

She liked the train that flew under the earth. She liked the way people crowded inside, bumping together as they clung to metal straps. There were colorful drawings to study and read. Some spoke of magical liquid that gifted the user with shiny, sexy hair. Another advised her to practice safe sex. There was a wall map provided for lost travelers, and yet another picture that boasted its elixir could transform the skin to make it sexually attractive to others.

Kadra leaned close to Harper's ear. 'Is sex the religion of your world?'

'Ah . . . you could say a lot of people worship it. Why are you whispering?'

'No one is speaking. Is conversation permitted?'

'Sure. It's just that most of these people don't know each other. They're strangers, so they don't have anything to say.'

Kadra considered it, and finding it reasonable, she tapped the shoulder of the woman standing beside her. 'I am Kadra, Slayer of Demons. My companion in this dimension is Harper Doyle. Together we hunt Sorak.'

The sound Harper made was somewhere between a laugh and a moan. 'Rehearsing,' he said with what he hoped was a nonthreatening smile. 'New play. Way, *way* off Broadway. Honey,' Harper said to Kadra as the woman edged as far away as the press of bodies would allow, 'maybe you should just talk to me.'

'Making introductions is courteous.'

'Yeah, well, you start chatting about demons, it tends to weird people out.'

The train stopped. People poured off, people poured on.

Kadra scowled and planted her feet. 'As you said, how can they defend against Sorak if they are unaware of him?'

'I've thought about that. Thought about going to the cops. The National Guard.' Frustrated, he dragged a hand through his hair. 'Nobody's going to believe us, and the time we'd waste trying to convince them we're not candidates for a padded cell would only give Sorak more of an advantage.'

'You said there were demons in this world, that you put them in cages.'

'There are plenty of them. But they're a different type than you're used to fighting. They're not another species, they're us. People come in a variety pack, Kadra. Most of them are good – at the core, they're good. But a lot of them aren't. So they prey on their own kind.'

'To prey on your own kind is the greatest sin. You hunt these demons. Who else hunts them?'

'Ideally? The law. It just doesn't always work out. It'll take more than a subway ride for me to explain it to you. I don't always understand it myself.'

'There is good and there is evil. The good must always fight the evil as the strong must always protect the weak. This is nothing that can change by walking through a portal.'

He linked his hand with hers. Her vision was so clear, he

thought. And her spirit so pure. 'I love you,' he murmured. 'I love everything about you.'

The warmth poured into her, flooding her belly, over-flowing her heart. 'You only know one day of me.'

'Time doesn't mean a damn.' The train jerked to a halt at the next station. 'We'll be getting off soon. Whatever happens tonight, I need you to believe what I'm telling you now. I love you. My world was incomplete until you came into it.'

'I believe what you say.' It felt strange and right to press her lips to his. 'My heart is joined to yours.'

But what she didn't say, what she couldn't bear to say, was that her world would be forever incomplete when she left him.

'You're thinking that when this is over, we won't be able to be together.' He put his hand on her cheek now, kept his gaze steady on hers. 'That I'll have to stay in this world, and you'll have to go back to yours.'

'There is only one thing that should be occupying our minds now. That is Sorak.'

'When we get off this train, we'll worry about Sorak. Right now, it's you and me.'

'You have a very domineering nature. I find it strangely appealing.'

'Same goes. When this is over, Kadra, we'll find a way. That's what people do when they love each other. They find a way.'

She thought of the globe in her pouch. The key that was hers only until the battle was done. The weight of it dragged on her heart like a stone. 'And when there is no way to be found?'

'Then they make one. Whatever I have to do to make it work, I'll do. But I won't lose you.'

'I can't stay in your world, Harper. I am a slayer, bound by blood, by oath, and by honor to protect my people.'

'Then I'll go with you.'

Stunned, she stared at him. 'You would give up your world, the wonders of it, for me? For mine?'

'For us. I'll do whatever has to be done to have a life with you.'

Tears swam into her eyes. She would never have shed one for pain, but one spilled down her cheek now. For love. 'It is not possible. It would never be permitted.'

'Who the hell's in charge? We'll have ourselves a sit-down.'

She managed a wobbly smile. 'It would take more than a subway ride to explain it to you. There are balances, Harper, that must be carefully held. I am here to right a wrong, and am given entrance by the power of Rhee's magic. When I have done what I've been sent here to do, I'll have no choice but to return. You will have no choice but to stay.'

'We'll just see about that. Here's our stop.'

'You are angry.'

'No, this isn't my angry face. This is my if-I-can-fight-demons-I-can-sure-as-hell-fight-the-cosmos face.' He gave her hand a squeeze. 'Trust me.'

She trusted no one more. If she had been permitted to take a lifemate, it would have been Harper Doyle. His strength, his honesty, his courage had stolen her heart. She would miss, for the rest of her life, his strange humor, his bravery, his skilled mouth.

When they had defeated Sorak, she would go quickly and spare them both the pain of leaving. And now she would treasure the time they had left as companions. She would relish the great deed they were fated to accomplish together.

The first order of business, Harper thought, was to get down on the tracks and into the tunnels while avoiding detection by the subway cops. He explained the problem to Kadra as they moved down the platform away from the bulk of the waiting commuters.

'Very well,' she said, and solved the dilemma by jumping down onto the tracks.

'Or we could do it that way,' he grumbled. He flashed his ID in the direction of a couple of gawking businessmen. 'Transit inspectors.'

Hoping they subscribed to the New York credo of minding their own business, he jumped. 'Move fast.' He took her arm. 'Stay out of the light. Once we're into the tunnels our main goal is to avoid being smeared on the tracks by an oncoming train. Then there's the third-rail factor. See that?' He pointed. 'Whatever you do, don't step on that, don't touch it. It'll fry you like a trout.'

He pulled his penlight from his pocket as they followed the track into the tunnel. 'There are some areas in the system where homeless people set up housekeeping.'

'If they have a house to keep, they cannot be homeless.'

'We'll save the tutorial on society's disenfranchised for later. Some of the people who manage to live down here are mentally unstable. Some are just desperate. What we're looking for, I figure, are the maintenance areas. Off the main tracks, where there's room to establish a lair.'

'There is no scent of people or demon here.'

'Let me know when that changes.' He felt the vibration, saw the first flicker of light in the dark. 'Train. Let's move.'

He doubled his pace toward the recess of an access door, and pulling her up with him, he plastered himself to the door. 'Think thin,' he advised.

He held on as the roar of the train blasted the air, gritted his teeth as the air pummeled them. Through the train's lighted windows, faces and bodies of its passengers blurred by.

'It is more exciting to be outside the box as it flies by than to be inside it.'

He looked over at Kadra as the last car whizzed past. 'One of these days you'll have to tell me what you do for entertainment back in A'Dair. I have a feeling I'll be riveted.'

He tried to keep a map in his head as they wound through the labyrinth. Twice more they were forced to leap for a narrow shelter as a train sped past. But it was Kadra who swung toward a side tunnel.

'Here. Sorak has been this way.'

Harper caught no scent in the stale air other than the grease and metal of machines. 'Can you tell how long ago?'

'Some hours past, but fresh enough to track.'

She moved carefully, knowing the dangers of an underground ruled by a demon. She kept her voice low as they began to hunt. 'The Bok sees as well in the dark as in the light. Perhaps better. He will fight more fiercely for his lair than he would even for food.'

'In other words, that skirmish we had this morning was just a preview of coming attractions.'

She thought she was beginning to understand his odd expressions, so nodded. 'Tonight, it is to the death.'

She whirled, coat billowing, as she laid a hand on the hilt of her sword. Though he had heard no sound, the beam of Harper's light picked out a shadow in the dark. He'd nearly drawn his gun when he recognized the uniform.

'Transit cop.' He said it under his breath to Kadra. 'Let me handle this. Hey, Officer. Riley and Tripp from the *Post*. We're cleared to do a feature on —'

He broke off as the figure took one shambling step toward him and his stiletto-like teeth gleamed in the narrow beam of light.

The teeth parted, row after monstrous row. The hands, tipped with bluing claws, lifted. But the eyes – the eyes were still painfully human.

'Help me. Please, God, help me.' And with a sound trapped between a sob and a howl, he leaped.

Kadra's dagger shot through the air and into his throat with an ugly sound of steel piercing flesh. The blood that trickled out of the wound was a thin reddish green.

'The change was not complete with this one,' Kadra stated.

'He was still human.' Furious, Harper dropped to his knees and tried to find a pulse. 'Goddamn it, he was still a human being. He was a fucking cop. You killed him without a thought.'

'He was neither human nor demon, but trapped between. I ended his life to save yours.'

'Is that all there is?' Harper's head whipped around, and his gaze burned into hers. 'Life or death? He asked for help.'

'I gave him the only help I could. Do you think it gives me pleasure? With his death, one of my people dies. That is the balance.' She crouched, pulled his dagger free. 'That is the price.'

'We could have gotten him to the hospital. A blood transfusion, something.'

'That is fantasy!' She shot her dagger home. 'He was dead the instant Sorak kissed him.' She gestured toward the body as it began to smoke. 'Infected with demon blood. There was nothing to be done for him, in your world or in mine. If Sorak has found one human to change, he has changed others.'

She glanced toward the dark maw of tunnel. She would rather face it, even if her own death waited inside, than the hot accusation in his eyes. 'If you are unable to do what must be done, go back now. I will go on alone.'

'He asked for help. He was scared. I saw the fear.' Now all Harper could see was a blackened skeleton. 'And he never had a chance.' Sickened, Harper got to his feet. 'We'll finish it together.'

'This is the way. I smell blood, some still fresh.' She walked deeper into the tunnel.

8

They moved in the dark, guided by the thin beam of Harper's penlight and Kadra's instincts. And they moved in silence.

She had killed a man – and to Harper the charred remains they had left behind in the tunnel were still a man. She had done so with the same cold efficiency she had used to destroy the hideous little two-headed monster in A'Dair.

In the zoo he'd found her brutal focus fascinating,

admirable. Even sexy. But there they had fought beasts — savage and hungry and alien despite their form.

This had been a man. How could she be so certain that his lunge forward had been an attack instead of a plea?

'You said it takes time for the transformation,' Harper began.

'In my world.' She snapped the words out. 'I can't know — no one can know — how the change happens in yours. No demon has ever traveled from my world to yours until now. In A'Dair, the demon carries his victim off, into a lair. For twelve hours the human sleeps, a changing sleep that is like death. Only during this period is there any hope of being saved, and even that hope is small. Once the demon wakes, it is too late. The change is irreversible even if he is not complete. He is demon. And he feeds.'

'If there's a different time frame here, maybe there's a different structure to the change.'

'He waked. He walked. He would have fed on you if he had not been stopped. The blood was already mixed, Harper. His death was a mercy. What was still human inside knew.'

She hadn't known love could be painful. She hadn't known that when your heart lay open to another it could be so easily wounded. But hers was, and the hurt ran down to the bone: he had looked at her as if she were the monster.

She didn't want to speak of it. She wished to push it aside and do only what she had come to do. But the ache in her heart was a distraction.

'Every human death is a death inside me.' She spoke quietly, without looking at him. 'I cannot save them all. I would give my life if that would make it otherwise.'

'I know that.' But they both heard the doubt in his voice.

The pain of it sliced through her, made her careless, made her vulnerable to what leaped at her out of the dark.

It was snarling, teeth snapping. Its claws swiped, scoring her neck as she whirled to block.

It was old and female. And it was mad. It skittered back, impossibly fast, like a spider, into the shadows. Kadra freed her sword and, going by scent and sound, struck out.

It cackled. That was the only way to describe the sound it made as it attacked Kadra from behind.

Harper's bullet caught it in midair. Blood gushed, that awful hue of mixed red and green, as it thudded to the ground, arms and legs drumming.

An old woman, Harper thought as he stared into the crazed and dying face. One of the pitiful who so often slipped through society's fingers and into its bowels.

She was old enough to be his grandmother.

'You did not kill her.' Kadra crouched beside him. 'You did not end her life, and you must not take the weight of it. Sorak killed her, and you ended her torment. You slayed the monster. The woman was already dead.'

'Do you get used to it?'

She hesitated, nearly lied. But when he lifted his head and looked into her eyes, she gave him the truth. 'Yes. You must, or how could you pick up your sword day after day? But there is regret, Harper. There is sorrow for what is lost. The demon has no regret, no sorrow. No joy or passion, no love. I think when they feed on us, they hope to consume what it is that makes us human. Our heart, our soul. But they cannot. All they can take and transform is the body. The heart and soul live on in another place. And that place is locked to them.'

'So Sorak's come here. Maybe he thinks he'll have better luck eating souls in this dimension.'

'Perhaps.'

The woman was all but ashes when Harper looked at Kadra again. 'I'm sorry about before. I didn't want to believe it could happen, that we could be used this way. It was easier to blame you for stopping it than Sorak for starting it.'

'There will be more.'

'And we'll both stop it.' He reached out, touched a fingertip to the claw marks on her neck. 'You're hurt.'

'Scratches, because I was careless. I won't be a second time.'

'Neither will I.' Not with the battle, he thought, and not with her. He took her hand as they got to their feet. 'Let's find this bastard, and welcome him to New York.'

Harper kept his Glock in one hand, the knife in the other. The tunnel curved, and a dim light glowed at the end of it. He heard the rumble of a train behind them, but ahead there was silence.

He could see signs of human habitation now. Broken glass, an empty pint bottle that had held cheap whiskey. Food wrappers, an old tennis shoe with the toe ripped out.

'His lair.' Gesturing with her chin, Kadra slid her sword out of its sheath. 'He is not alone.'

'Well, why don't we join the party?' He turned the knife in his hand. 'We've brought our host some nice gifts.'

She stripped off the coat, flung it aside. 'He will not be pleased to see us.'

The tunnel widened. There was more debris from the life that had chosen to spread underground. Spoiled food, battered boxes that might have served as shelter. A headless doll. And as they drew closer to the light, a splatter of blood against the dingy wall.

The first three came out in a mad rush, all claws and teeth. Harper fired, sweeping his aim left to right. There was a stench of something not human as one threw the wounded at Harper, then came in like a missile beneath the body. Its teeth fixed in his calf as he sliced upward with the knife.

The teeth continued to grip his leg like a vice even as the thing began to smoke. He cursed, kicked, and felt both cloth and flesh tear as the demi-demon struck the tunnel wall.

He spun clear to see that Kadra had already killed the third, and a fourth that had tried to use the cover of their attack for one of his own.

She wasn't even winded.

'That was too easy,' she commented.

'Yeah.' He limped over, gritting his teeth against the burning pain of the bite. 'That was a real breeze.'

'He toys with us.' Now she pulled out the healing cloth. 'He insults us. Bind your wound.'

He knelt, quickly tied the cloth around his bleeding leg. 'And just how is sending four advance men with really nasty teeth an insult?'

'He knew we would destroy them. Four, not fully changed, are child's play.'

'Yeah.' Grimly he tightened the knot on the cloth. 'I'm feeling real childlike at the moment.'

'He wants us in there. Wants to watch the battle. The smell of blood feeds him almost as much as the taste.'

'Okay.' He tested his weight on the injured leg. It would have to hold. 'Let's go give his majesty a real five-star meal.'

She drew her dagger, checked the balance of both blades, then nodded. 'For your world and for mine. To the death.'

'Let's make that Sorak's death.'

They charged.

Kadra caught a blur of movement above, and went into a roll that sent the demon flying over her head. She ran him through with one thrust, pulled her sword out clean before his body hit the ground. Using her hips, she reared up, shot her boots into the next attacker's face. And was on her feet, hacking and whirling.

She heard gunshots and, pivoting, saw Harper slay two demi-demons on his left and set to meet another on his right with his blade.

She spun clear, slicing with her sword, and positioned herself so they fought back-to-back.

'Sorak is close!' she shouted. 'I smell him.'

'Yeah.' Sweat dripped into Harper's eyes and was ignored. 'So do I.'

He shot a bony, bald demi-demon who still wore a torn

and faded New York Mets T-shirt. As the demon smoked and died at his feet, Harper scanned the tunnel.

He couldn't think about who they had been, he told himself, only what they had become.

'I don't see any more of them.'

Still back-to-back, they circled. 'Sorak!' Kadra shouted. 'Come and meet your fate.'

As if on cue, light flashed into the tunnel. Through the glare of it, three demons charged.

'He's used the portal. He's brought more through.'

Harper fired, and when the Glock clicked on empty, he used it as a club. His leg screamed as he sprang off it to launch himself into a roundhouse kick. The demon barely staggered, shoving Harper so that his wounded leg buckled. He skidded over the floor, and lost his breath and the gun when the demon landed on him.

For the second time, he felt the bite of claws. Screaming in rage, he plunged the knife into the demon's throat, snarled like an animal himself when the thick green spewed onto his hands and face.

When he crawled out, covered with blood, he saw Kadra fighting both of the remaining demons.

Her blades flashed like lightning. She blocked the sickle sword that one of them swung at her, then plunged her dagger into his belly while she hacked her blade through the second demon.

'Next time,' Harper said as he limped toward her, 'I get the two-on-one.'

Winded, she nodded. 'Next time.'

The smoking blood hazed the air. She peered through it, pointed her sword at Sorak. His claws and face were smeared with the blood of the body that lay at his feet.

He had fed, and fed again, she realized, and would have the strength of ten.

Still, her stance was cocky, her voice a sneer. 'You should have brought an army, demon king. We would have littered this place with your dead.'

'I brought better than an army.' Sorak reached back and hefted a small girl by the scruff of her neck. She let out a sobbing squeal as her little legs kicked in the air, two full feet off the ground.

Leering, Sorak skimmed his teeth over her throat. 'The young are so sweet to the taste. How much for her life?'

Kadra lowered her blade. Though her hand was steady, her heart stumbled in her chest. 'Will you bargain your life with a human child's? Is not a king worth more?'

'I was not speaking to you, Kadra, Slayer of Demons.' Sorak lifted his other hand, and the gun.

Subway cop, Harper thought on a jolt of panic. Sorak had taken the gun from the transit cop, and he had been too angry to notice the empty holster.

On an oath, Harper shoved Kadra aside as Sorak fired. As she fell, blood streaming from her temple, the sword clattered to the ground.

'No. Goddamn it, no!' Harper fell to his knees, gathering her up, checking quickly for a pulse.

'I was born for her death.' Sorak shook the child until she began to wail. 'Tell me, Harper Doyle, were you born for death?'

She was alive, he told himself. And slayers healed quickly. He would do whatever he could to give her that time, and to save an innocent child from death. Or worse.

He got to his feet, the knife gripped in his hand. 'For yours. I was born for yours.'

'Approach me and . . . ' Sorak ran a blue claw teasingly down the girl's round cheek as her wails became the mewling sounds of a trapped animal. 'I tear her to pieces. How much for the child, Harper Doyle? How much are the young worth in this world?'

Her eyes were blue, Harper noted. Glassy as a doll's now, filled with shock. 'How much do you want?'

'You will do. Your life for her life. I would enjoy taking

what is the slayer's and making it mine. Throw down your blade, or the child dies now.'

'And Kadra?'

Through the stinking smoke Harper saw the gleam of jagged teeth. 'Do you think your life is worth both of theirs?' Sorak stepped forward, and Harper could see blood coming from wounds of the claws sliding down the girl's white neck. 'I could kill you where you stand with this weapon. But it would be . . . unsporting. Make the bargain, or watch while I give her my kiss.'

There was no bargaining with monsters. Even knowing that, Harper could see no choice. 'Set her down, let her go. A knife isn't much good against a gun. You're smart enough to know that. In this world, using a kid as a shield is a sign of a coward. I thought you were a king.'

'I am more than king here. I am god.' Carelessly, he tossed the girl on the floor, then drew out the globe. The portal burst open. 'Run, little human child. Run quickly, or I will take you after all.'

She ran, weeping. The portal snapped shut behind her.

'And now.' Grinning, Sorak streaked forward in a move so fast that Harper had no chance to evade or defend. Using the back of his hand, Sorak struck Harper in the face with a blow so vicious that it threw Harper back against the wall. The knife spurted out of his hand like wet soap.

With the wall bracing him, Harper slid to the ground.

'You are mine now. A warrior slave in my army, in this world. I will rule here.'

'Fry in hell,' Harper choked out as those claws closed over his throat. In his mind, he called out to Kadra to wake, to save herself from the horror that was coming.

'Soon you will see what it is to be as I am. To lose those weaknesses that make you human.' Sorak leaned close, his mouth only a fetid breath away from Harper's, his gleaming teeth bared. 'I will give you the slayer when you wake, and we will feed on her together.'

He knew pain, agony beyond imagining as that mouth, those teeth closed over him. The shock of it ripped through his system, tore at his sanity as those keen blue claws tore through flesh until he felt his own heart prepare to burst.

The hand that had been fighting to reach the gun in his boot convulsed, dropped limply to the ground.

He had visions of fire and smoke, of blood and brutal death. Torment and anguish. With them came a lethargy that weighed his limbs down like molten lead.

Through the smoke, through the pain, he heard Kadra scream his name.

His trembling fingers closed over the gun. His numb arm moved, slowly, slowly, in exquisite pain to bring it between their bodies. Without being fully aware of where the muzzle was pointed, he fired.

9

When Kadra came to, her vision was smeared with blood and pain. Her body knew a thousand stings and aches from the battle. Her ears still rang from it.

And her first thought as she pushed to her knees was: Harper.

The air was clogged with smoke and stink from the blood of a dozen demons and demi-demons. She remembered the child and her heart jerked. Burying her pain, she picked up her sword, gripped it in both hands.

The sound she heard now, slicing through the filthy air, was one of greed, one of bitter glory. Whirling, she swung the sword high over her head.

She saw, huddled by the dripping wall, Sorak, his regal cape unstained as he gifted the bleeding Harper with his evil kiss.

Fear, rage, horror gushed through her and poured out in a single urgent cry that was Harper's name.

She ran, screaming still, the point of her blade pointing toward the ceiling, where it caught the dim light and glinted like vengeance.

The gunshot was a small sound, a muffled crack like the rap of a fist on wood. Sorak's body jerked, and his head lifted with a kind of baffled shock. He pressed a hand to his belly where his blood spilled between his slender blue-tipped fingers.

'I am king of the Bok.' Sorak watched in confusion as his own blood poured. 'I am god here. I cannot be destroyed by human means.'

'Wanna bet?' With what little strength he had left, Harper fired again. 'You lose,' he managed before his head slumped.

Kadra leaped between them as Sorak collapsed. She whipped her sword down, the point at its heart. 'He has killed you. Harper the warrior has sent you to hell.'

'And I have made him mine.' His grin spread. 'And you, Kadra, Slayer of Demons, must destroy what you love or be destroyed by it. I have won.'

'He will never be yours. That is my vow.' With all of her strength, she rammed the sword home. Leaving it buried in Sorak's body and in the stone beneath, she dropped to her knees beside Harper.

There was blood, his own and Sorak's, on his face. The healing cloth around his wounded leg had soaked through. His eyes were already going dim.

But they met Kadra's now with something like triumph. 'He's done.'

'Yes.' The slayer's fingers shook as she brushed Harper's hair from his face. 'He is finished.'

'Mission accomplished, huh? The kid.' He closed his eyes on a wave of agony, a flood of impossible fatigue. 'The kid got back through the portal.'

'You traded your life for hers.' For mine, she thought. And for mine.

'She couldn't've been more than two. I couldn't stand there and let him . . . Christ.' He had to gather strength just to breathe. 'Your head's bleeding.'

'It's only—'

'A scratch. Yeah, yeah. Got a few of my own.' He bore

down, fought to clear his vision so he could see her better. 'Baby, I'm pretty messed up here.'

'I will get you to a healer.'

'Kadra.' He wanted to take her hand, but couldn't lift his arm. 'Bastard kissed me. It works faster here, the change. We can't be sure how fast.'

'You will not change. You will *not*.' Tears ran down her cheeks unchecked. 'I will take you back, through the portal. To Rhee, the sorceress.'

'I'm going under. I can feel it.' He was cold, cold to the bone. Losing, he knew, the warmth of his own humanity. 'We can't take the chance. You know what you have to do.'

'No.' She gripped his face with desperate hands. 'No.'

'I dropped the gun. Get it for me, let me do it myself.'

'No.' She pressed his face to her breast and rocked. 'No, no, no.'

The smell of her flesh brought comfort, but under it, creeping under it, was an ugly, alien hunger that horrified him. 'Don't let me change. If you love me, end it. Let me die human.' He pressed his lips to her heart. 'I love you. Let that be the last thing we both remember from this. I love you.'

He went limp. Panic filled her, a wild weeping as she

shook him, slapped him, called to him. But he was in the changing sleep, a kind of living death, and could not be reached.

'No. You will not take him.' She leaped up, whirled to where Sorak had died. All that was left was her sword, still in the stone, and the globe the demon king had stolen. She scooped up the globe, then with a piercing battle cry, wrenched her sword free.

Tears streamed down her stony face as she dropped down beside Harper again, wrapped her arms around him.

But when the portal opened and the light burst over them, it took them to a world she had never seen.

The room was white. Through a wall of glass were trees of crimson and sapphire against a pale gold sky. Framed by it, robed in white, stood Rhee.

'Help him.' Kadra laid Harper between them, stretched out her arms in pleading. 'Save him.'

'I cannot.'

'You have power.'

'So do we all. Child—'

'Do not call me child.' Furious, primed for battle, Kadra leaped to her feet. 'Some are saved from the changing sleep through sorcery. I have heard the tales.'

'It is beyond my means to save him.'

'You say we share blood, but you refuse the one thing I have ever asked of you. You sent me to him.'

'Not I, but destiny.'

'Destiny,' Kadra spat out. 'Who weaves a destiny that asks a man to fight what is not his war, to risk his life in a battle not his own? This he did. He fought with me, and for me. He destroyed the Bok king when I failed. He laid down his life for a child who was not his own. And for this courage, for this valor, he is repaid by becoming what he fought against. Who asks such a sacrifice?'

'There are no answers to the questions you ask. What did he bring to you, what was your gift to him?'

'Love.'

'Then there is a way. Courage and strength,' Rhee said as she stepped forward. 'Vision and love. With these there is a way for you, only you, to save him.'

'How? Whatever it is, I will do. A quest, a battle? Tell me, and it is done.'

'A kiss.'

'A kiss?'

'A gift of breath, of life and love. If your love is true, if it is pure, one to the other, the power of that kiss, of the love in it, will overcome the evil of the demon's.'

'Can it be so simple?'

'Nothing ever is,' Rhee said with a smile. 'You must be cleansed first. I will help you, and tell you the rest.'

'There is no time.' Her heart lurched as she gestured to Harper. His fingernails were a pale blue. 'He is already changing.'

'Time stops here. That I can give you. He will remain as he is while we prepare.'

'There is choice,' Rhee said while Kadra bathed. 'There is great risk.'

'I am a warrior,' Kadra replied.

'You must be woman and warrior now.'

'So I bathe in scented oils, wash my hair with jasmine blossoms. I have no patience for such matters.'

'Rituals.' Rhee's lips curved as she held out a thick white towel. 'Do you not sharpen your sword before battle? This is not so different. Not all warriors are female, daughter, but all females should be warriors. He will need all you are if he is to survive this.'

'If I fail, may he stay here? Sleep, as he is sleeping now?'

Gently, Rhee touched Kadra's hair. 'Would you wish that for him? An eternity of nothing?'

'I cannot let him change. It was the last thing he asked of me, to take his life so he might end it as a man.'

'And will you?'

'I will not let him die a beast. I will not fail him. If I use my sword to end it, I will never lift it again.'

This, Rhee thought, was what I wished for you. Beyond valor and might, beyond battle cries and quests, a love so deep it is a drowning pool.

'These are choices that only you can make. There is one more. The magic that passed from my blood to yours is strong. But more potent is the magic you found in your own heart. Trust it.'

Rhee closed her hands around her daughter's arms. Arms, she thought now, that had learned to lift a sword and to embrace a man who was her equal. 'Give yourself to it without hesitation. If you waver, if you doubt and still do this thing, he may live. You may not.'

Rhee offered a long white robe. 'Wear this.'

'Strange garb for battling life and death.' Kadra put it on, belted it. 'If my love isn't strong enough, I die.'

Rhee folded her hands because they longed to reach out, to touch, to soothe. 'Yes. I gave you to your fate once before. And my arms ached from emptiness. I watched you, in my way, as you grew, as you became. And I was proud. But my arms were empty. Now, I give you once more to your fate.'

'Did you love the man who was my father?'

'With everything I am. And yet I could not save him. I could only watch while he was taken from me. He would have been proud, as I am, of the life we made together in you.'

'Mother,' Kadra said when Rhee turned to the arched opening. And she stepped forward, let herself be gathered close. Let herself hold.

'You found kindness,' Rhee murmured. 'And forgiveness. They will make you stronger.' She held tight one moment more, just one moment more. 'Be strong, my daughter. It is time.'

She led Kadra back into the white room. Now Harper lay on a bed that was draped with thin white curtains. A garden of white flowers surrounded it. Dozens of slender, milky tapers added a quiet light.

He wore a white shirt and trousers. His face, while deathly pale, was unmarked.

Kadra parted the bed curtains. 'His wounds.'

'This much I could do. His flesh is healed, as yours is.'

'He is beautiful. He is . . . ' My life, she thought. 'I have only known him a day, yet he has changed me forever.'

'You changed each other. And that change will be stronger than the one Sorak put inside him. You must believe it.'

'A sword is not enough.' Kadra glanced over. 'Is this my lesson?'

'You have always had more than a sword. Sorak is dead. Together you have accomplished this great feat, and both our worlds are safe. For this gift, each of you is granted passage into both worlds. As you choose.'

'How can this be? The balance—'

'Love makes its own balance.' Rhee walked to a table where each of the globes stood on a small pedestal. One emerald, one ruby.

'The emerald is your stone, and its key opens the portal to the world you knew. The ruby is his, and its key opens to his world. I must leave you. What you do now is between only you two. I will always be with you. Kadra, Slayer of Demons, your fate is again in your own hands.'

Rhee held up her arms and vanished.

'This I must do without sword or dagger.' Still, she took her circlet from the table, placed it on her scented hair. 'But I am what I am. And all I am is yours, Harper Doyle.'

She stepped to the bed, placed a hand on his cold cheek. The words were inside her, as if they, too, had been sleeping. 'I love you with heart, with soul, with body. In all worlds, in all times. Come back to me.'

And bending, she laid her lips on his.

Love and life, she thought as she breathed both into his mouth. Life and love. Strong as a stallion, pure as a dove. She drew the poison in, gave him her breath. Gift of heart and soul take now from me, and from the Demon Kiss be free.

Pain vibrated through her, but she kept her lips warm and gentle on his. Dizzy, she braced a hand beside his head, and gave.

I would die for you, she thought. I would live for you.

When his mouth moved under hers, when he stirred, she slid bonelessly to her knees beside the bed.

Outside, the sky deepened, gleamed gold, and the jeweled trees shimmered.

Harper dreamed of swimming, fighting through a black and churning sea that was swallowing him whole. He broke through its icy void, searching for her, battling the greedy waves that sucked him back.

Until he slid into a warm white river, floated there. And woke speaking her name.

She lifted her head, and felt no shame at the tears as she gripped his hand. 'Yes. Yes, yes.' She pressed his hand to her cheek, kissed it, then taking his hand, she laughed in relief at the healthy color in his skin and nails. 'Baby,' she said, relishing the term, 'I am with you.'

He saw only white, the gauzy draperies, the glow of

candles through them, the richness of the flowers. Then he saw her as she rose up beside him and again laid her lips on his.

'If this is hell,' he said aloud, 'it's not so bad.'

'You are not dead. You live. You are unchanged.'

He sat up, amazed at the energy running through him, the absolute freedom from pain. 'How?'

'Love was enough.'

'Works for me. Where are we? What did you do?'

'We're in yet another dimension. Rhee the sorceress . . . my mother, brought us. She healed us.'

'And what, exorcised the demon?'

'That was for me. A kiss waked you, and brought you back whole.'

'Like Sleeping Beauty? You're kidding.'

She leaned back. 'You look displeased.'

'Well, Jesus, it's embarrassing.' He scooped his hair back, slid off the bed.

'You would rather die, with pride?' Though part of her understood the sentiment perfectly well, it still rankled. She who had never believed in romance had found the event desperately romantic. The kind of moment the bards write of. 'You are ungrateful and stupid.'

'Stupid, maybe. Ungrateful, definitely not. But if it's all

the same to you, let's just keep this one portion of the experience completely to ourselves.'

She jerked a shoulder, lifted her chin. And made him smile. 'You saved my life, and you made me a man. Thank you.'

Now she sniffed. 'You are a brave warrior and did not deserve the fate Sorak intended for you.'

'There you go. My ego's nearly back to normal now. And can I just say you look gorgeous. Incredible. In fact, there's an expression in my world about how you look right now. It goes something like, wow.'

'Ritual foolishness,' she replied, flipping a hand at the robe.

'I love the way you look. I love you, Kadra.'

She sighed. 'I know. If the love between us was not strong and true, you would not have waked so I could be annoyed with you.' She looked away from him, deliberately, when he came to her, when he wrapped his arms tight around her.

So he kissed her cheek, kissed her temple where a bullet had grazed. 'I thought I had lost you, and that was worse than thinking I'd lost myself.'

Yielding, she turned her lips to his. 'Harper Doyle.'

'Kadra, Slayer of Demons.'

She eased back, her eyes solemn despite the humor in his. 'Do you wish me to be your lifemate and bear your young?'

'You bet I do.'

'This is what I wish as well. This is not a traditional path for a slayer.'

He lifted a hand to skim a finger over her circlet of rank. 'We'll make new traditions. Stay with me, Kadra. Be with me. We'll stay here, wherever this is. It doesn't matter.'

'This is not our place.' She stepped back, gestured to the two globes. 'The one on the emerald stand opens to my world. The ruby to yours. I believed that to keep the balance we must each go back, must each remain in the world where we came from. But, I have vision.'

She looked back at him. 'My mother is a sorceress, and her blood is my blood. I see what I once refused to see. I have magic inside me. I must practice with this as I once practiced with a sword. Until I am skilled.'

'Slayer and sorceress. I get a two-for-one.'

'There can be no balance when love is denied and refused. We are meant, so we will be.'

'Choose,' he told her. 'I'll live in any world, as long as it's with you.'

She picked up the bag that held their things, tossed it to

him. She lifted her sword. And, crossing to the table, she lifted the globe that rested on a ruby stand.

'The Bok have lost their king, and the slayers who are my sisters will rout them, and continue the fight against all demons. But there are battles to be fought in your world, demons of a different kind to be vanquished. I wish to fight with you there.'

'Partners, then.' He took her hand, kissed it. 'We make a hell of a team.'

'And I like the pie called pizza, and the beer. And even more than these, the kissing.'

'Baby, we were made for each other.'

He swung her into his arms, crushed his lips to hers. When the portal opened, and the light washed in, they leaped into it together.

And went home.

THE WITCHING HOUR

Prologue

In a distant time, in a distant place, the great island of Twylia swam in the vast blue Sea of Wonders. It was a land of mountains and valleys, of green forests and silver rivers, of wide fertile fields and quiet lakes. To those who lived there, it was the whole of the world.

Some said that once, in the dawn of beginnings, there was a bridge of land that led to other worlds, and back again to Twylia. A bridge of rock and earth conjured by the great wizard-god Draco, and so destroyed by him when the world beyond became a battlefield of greed and sorrow.

For on Twylia peace and prosperity prevailed for a thousand seasons.

But a time came when men – some men – sought more. When the more they sought was riches not earned, women not wooed, land not honored. And power, most of all – power not respected.

With this avarice, war and death, treachery and fear infected Twylia so that Draco, and those who came from him, wept to see the green fields stained with blood and the valleys echoing with the cries of starving children. He vowed, as he stood on the peak of Sorcerer's Mountain, in the light of the moon, on the night of the solstice, that peace would return to the world.

It would come through blood, and courage, through pure love and willing sacrifice. After dark days, the light would shine again. And so he cast his spell.

There will be one born in the darkest hour of the darkest night who will wield the power and bring the light. The Crown of Stars only one will wear to prove this be my one true heir. Through blood and valor, through grief and joy, the True One shields what greed would destroy. But one seeks another, woman to man, heart to heart, and hand to hand. So warrior, witch, daughter, and son, will complete what has begun. If there is strength and hearts are pure, this land of Twylia will endure.

The midnight hour will forge their power to free this world of tyranny. As I will, so mote it be.

From the peak of Sorcerer's Mountain, to the Valley of Faeries far below, across the fields and lakes and forests, the length and breadth of the island trembled from the might of the spell. Wind swirled and lightning spat.

So Draco sat atop his mountain and watched in glass and fire, in star and water as years passed.

As Draco bided, the world struggled. Good against evil, hope against despair. Magic dimmed in all but the secret places, and some grew to fear as much as covet it.

For a time, a short time, light bloomed again when good Queen Gwynn took the throne. The blood of the sorcerer ran in her veins, as did his love for the world. She was fair of face and of heart and ruled with a firm and loving hand beside her husband, the warrior-king Rhys. Together, they worked to heal the world, to rebuild the once grand City of Stars, to make the forests and fertile valleys safe again for the people of the world.

Hope shimmered into light, but its opposite lurked, and plotted. The shadows of envy and greed slithered in the corners and the caves of Twylia. And those shadows, under the guise of peace and reconciliation, armed for war and treachery. They marched into the City of Stars on a cold

December morning, led by Lorcan, whose mark was the snake. And he would be king at any cost.

Blood and smoke and death followed. Come the dawn, the valiant Rhys lay dead and many who had fought with him slaughtered. Of the queen there was no sign.

On the eve of the solstice, Lorcan proclaimed himself king of Twylia and celebrated in the great hall of the castle, where royal blood stained the stones.

1

Snow fell in streams of icy white. It chilled to the bone, but she didn't curse it. It would blind any who pursued, and cover the trail. The bitter white cold was a blessing.

Her heart was broken, and her body nearly done. But she could not, would not yield. Rhys spoke to her, a spirit whisper in her mind that urged her to be strong.

She did not weep for his death. The tears, a woman's tears for the man she loved, were frozen inside her. She did not cry out against the pain, though the pain was great. She was more than a woman. More even than a witch.

She was a queen.

Her mount plowed through the snow, surefooted and loyal. As loyal, she knew, as the man who rode in silence beside her. She would need the loyalty of the faithful Gwayne, for she knew what was coming, what she could not stop. Though she hadn't seen her beloved Rhys's death, she knew the instant the usurper's sword had struck him down. So inside her cold and shattered heart she was prepared for what was to come.

She bit back a moan as the pain tore through her, breathed fast through her teeth until it eased again and she could say what needed to be said to Gwayne's silence.

'You could not have saved him. Nor could I.' Tears stung her eyes and were viciously willed away. 'Nor could I,' she said again. 'You served him, and me, by obeying his last order to you. I regret ... I'm sorry that I made it difficult for you to do so.'

'I am the queen's man, my lady.'

She smiled a little. 'And so you will continue to be. Your king thought of me. Even in the heat of battle, he thought of me, and our world. And our child.' She pressed a hand to her heavy belly, to the life that beat there. 'They will sing songs of him long after ...' The pain ripped a gasp from her, had her fumbling the reins.

'My lady!' Gwayne grabbed her reins to steady her mount. 'You cannot ride.'

'I can. I will.' She turned her head, and her eyes were a fierce and angry green in a face as pale as the snow. 'Lorcan will not find my child. It's not time. It's not yet time. There will be a light.' Exhausted, she slumped over the neck of her horse. 'You must watch for the light, and guide us to it.'

A light, Gwayne thought, as they trudged through the forest. Night was falling, and they were miles from the City of Stars, miles from any village or settlement he knew. Nothing lived in these woods but faeries and elves, and what good were they to a soldier and a woman – queen or no – who was great with child?

But here, into the Lost Forest, was where she'd ordered him to take her. She'd fought him, that was true enough, when he bowed to the king's command and dragged her from the castle. He had no choice but to lift her bodily onto the horse and whip her mount into a run.

They fled from the battle, from the stench of smoke and blood, from the screams of the dying. And royal command or not, he felt a coward for being alive while his king, his people, his friends were dead.

Still, he would guard the queen with his sword, with his

shield, with his life. When she was safe, he would go back. He would slay the murderous Lorcan, or die trying.

There was murmuring under the wind, but it was nothing human, so didn't concern him. Magic didn't worry him. Men did. There may have been sorcery in Lorcan's ambush, but it was men who had carried it out. It had been lies as much as spells that had opened the doors for him, allowed him to walk into the castle under the flag of diplomacy.

And all the while his men – those as vicious as he, and others he'd gathered from the far edges of the world and paid to fight in his name, – had prepared for the slaughter.

Not war, Gwayne thought grimly. It wasn't war when men slit the throats of women, stabbed unarmed men in the back, killed and burned for the joy of it.

He glanced toward the queen. Her eyes stared straight ahead, but seemed blind to him. As if, he thought, she was in some sort of trance. He wondered why she hadn't seen the deception, the bloodbath to come. Though he was a queen's man in spite of her reputed powers rather than because of them, he figured sorcerer's blood should have some vision.

Maybe it had something to do with her condition. He didn't know anything about increasing women, either. He hadn't wed, and didn't intend to. He was a soldier, and in his mind a soldier had no need of wiving.

And what would he do when the time came for the babe? He prayed to every god who walked or flew that the queen would know what to do – in the way he assumed a woman knew of such matters.

The heir to Twylia born in a snowbank in the Lost Forest during a winter storm. It wasn't right. It wasn't seemly.

And it terrified him more than any enemy's sword.

They must stop soon, for their mounts were near exhaustion. He would do what he could to make a shelter for her. Build a fire. Then, gods willing, things would . . . progress as nature demanded they progress.

When it was done, and they'd rested, he would get them – somehow – to the Valley of Secrets, and the settlement of women – some said enchantresses – who lived there.

The queen and the child would be safe, and he would go back – go back and drive his sword through Lorcan's throat.

He heard a sound – it was like music through the soughing wind. And looking to the west, he saw a glimmer of light through the stormy dark.

'My lady! A light.'

'Yes. Yes. Hurry. There isn't much time.'

He pushed the mounts off the path, so they were forced to wade through the sea of snow, to wind around ice-sheathed trees toward that small flicker of light. The wind brought the smell of smoke to him, and his fingers gripped the hilt of his sword.

Ghosts slipped out of the dark, with arrows notched.

He counted six, and his soldier's sense warned him there were more. 'We have no gold,' he shouted. 'We have nothing to steal.'

'That's your misfortune.' One of the ghosts stepped forward, and he saw it a was a man. Only a man, and a Traveler at that. 'Why do you journey here, and on such a night?'

Travelers might steal, Gwayne knew, for the sport of it. But they wouldn't attack unprovoked, and their reputation for hospitality was as renowned as their love of the road.

'Our business is our own, and we want no trouble from you, but only some of the warmth of your fire. I have a lady with me. She is near her time. She needs women to help her with the birthing.'

'Throw down your sword.'

'I will not. Nor will I raise it against you unless you seek to harm my lady. Even a Traveler should honor and respect a woman about to give birth.'

The man grinned, and under his hood his face was

brown as a nut and just as hard. 'Even a soldier should honor and respect men with arrows pointed at his heart.'

'Enough.' Gwynn threw her hood back, gathered her strength to raise her voice. 'I am Gwynn, Queen of Twylia. Have you not seen the portents even through the storm of snow? Have you not seen the black snake slither over the sky this night to snuff out the stars?'

'We have seen, Majesty.' The man and those with him lowered to one knee in the snow. 'My wife, our wise-woman, told us to wait, to watch for you. What has happened?'

'Lorcan has overthrown the City of Stars. He has murdered your king.'

The man rose, laid a fist on his heart. 'We are not warriors, my lady queen, but if you bid it, we will arm and band and march against the snake in your name.'

'So you will, but not tonight, and not in my name but in the name of one yet to come. Your name, sir?'

'I am Rohan, my lady.'

'Rohan of the Travelers, I have sought you for a great task, and now I ask your help, for without it, all is lost. This child seeks to be born. Draco's blood runs through me, and through this baby. You share this blood. Will you help me?'

'My lady, I and all I have are yours to command.' He took

her horse's halter. 'Go back,' he shouted to one of his men. 'Tell Nara and the women to prepare for a birth. A royal birth,' he added, his teeth flashing in a smile. 'We welcome a cousin.' He pulled the horse toward the camp. 'And enjoy a fight. Though Travelers pay little mind to the changing wind of politics, you will find none among us who has love for Lorcan.'

'Politics play no part in murder done under a flag of truce. And your fate is tied to what happens this night.'

He looked back at her and fought off a shudder. It seemed her eyes burned through the dark and into him. 'I give you my sympathies for the loss of your husband.'

'It is more than that.' She reached down, gripped his hand with an urgency that ground bone to bone. 'You know the Last Spell of Draco?'

'Everyone knows it, my lady. The song of it is passed generation to generation.' And he, a man who feared little, felt his hand tremble in hers. 'This child?'

'This child. This night. It is destiny, and we must not fail to meet it.'

The pain seized her, and she swooned. She heard voices, dim and distant. A hundred voices, it seemed, rising up in a flood. Hands reached for her, lifted her down from her mount as the birth pangs ripped a cry from her throat.

She smelled pine, and snow and smoke, felt something cool pressed to her brow. When she came back to herself, she saw a young woman with bright red hair that gleamed in the firelight. 'I am Rhiann, sister of Rohan. Drink a little, my lady. It will ease you.'

She sipped from the cup held to her lips and saw she was in a rough shelter of branches. A fire burned nearby. 'Gwayne?'

'Your man is just outside, my lady.'

'This is women's work, and men are useless here, be they warrior or scholar.'

'My mother,' Rhiann said. 'Nara.'

Gwynn looked at the woman busily tearing cloth. 'I'm grateful to you.'

'Let's get this baby into the world, such as it is, then you can be grateful. Get that water on the fire. Fetch my herbs.' The orders were snapped out as Gwynn felt the grip of the next pang.

Through the blurring of her vision she saw movement, heard chatter. More women. Women's work. Birth was the work of women, and death, it seemed, the work of men. Tears she'd conquered earlier now began to spill.

More voices spoke to her, inside her head, and told her what she already knew. But they were small comfort as she fought to give her child life.

'Midnight approaches.' She turned her head against Rhiann's bracing shoulder. 'The solstice. The darkest hour of the darkest day.'

'Push,' Nara ordered. 'Push!'

'The bells, the bells strike the hour.'

'There are no bells here, my lady.' Rhiann watched the cloths go red with blood. Too much blood.

'In the City of Stars, Lorcan has the bells rung. For his celebration, he thinks. But they ring out for the child, for the beginning. Oh! Now!'

Rearing back, she pushed the child into life. She heard the cries and laughed through her own weeping.

'This is her hour, this is her time. The witching hour between night and day. I must hold her.'

'You're weak, my lady.' Nara passed the squalling baby to Rhiann.

'You know as well as I, I'm dying. Your skill, Nara, your herbs, even your magic can't stop my fate. Give me my child.'

She held out her arms, and smiled at Rhiann. 'You have a kind heart to weep for me.'

'My lady.'

'I must speak to Gwayne. Quickly,' she said as Rhiann put the baby in her arms. 'There's little time. Ah, there you are. There you are, my sweet girl.' She pressed a kiss on the baby's head. 'You've healed my heart, and now it tears in two again. Part to stay here with you, part to go to your father. How I grieve to leave you, my own. You will have his eyes, and his courage. My mouth, I think,' she murmured and kissed it, 'and what runs in my blood. So much depends on you. Such a small hand to hold the world.'

She smiled over the baby's head. 'She will need you,' she said to Nara. 'You will teach her what women need to know.'

'You would put your child into the hands of a woman you don't know?'

'You heard the bells.'

Nara opened her mouth, then sighed. 'Yes, I heard them.' And she had seen, with a woman's heavy heart, what would pass this night.

Gwayne came into the shelter, fell to his knees beside her. 'My lady.'

'She is Aurora. She is your light, your queen, your charge. Will you swear your fealty to her?'

'I will. I do.'

'You cannot leave her.'

'My lady, I must—'

'You cannot go back. You must swear to me to stay beside her. Keep her safe. You must swear on my blood that you will protect her as you have protected me.' She took his hand, laid it on the child. 'Gwayne, my white hawk. You are hers now. Swear it.'

'I swear it.'

'You will teach her what a warrior needs to know. She will stay with the Travelers. Hidden in the hills, and in the shadows of the forest. When it is time . . . you will know, you will tell her what she is.' She turned the child so he could see the birthmark, a pale star, on the baby's right thigh. 'All she is. Until then, Lorcan must not know of her. He will want her death above all things.'

'I will guard her, on my life.'

'She has her hawk, and her dragon watches from the highest point of the world,' she murmured. 'Her wolf will come when he's needed. Oh, my heart, my own.' She pressed her lips to the child's cheeks. 'This is why I was born, why I loved, why I died. And still, I grieve to leave you.' She drew a trembling breath. 'I give her into your hands.' She held the baby out to Gwayne.

Then she held out her own, palms up. 'I still have something left in me. She will have it.' Light spun over her hands, whirled and caught the red, the gold from the fire. Then with a flash, what lay in Gwynn's hands became a star and a moon, both clear as ice.

'Keep them for her,' she said to Nara.

The good queen closed her eyes and slipped away. The young queen wailed in the arms of a grieving soldier.

2

Seasons passed, and the world suffered under the harsh reign of King Lorcan. Small rebellions were crushed with a brutality that washed the land with blood and sent even the valiant into hiding. Faeries, witches, seers, and all who dwelt within the Realm of Magicks were outlawed and hunted like wild beasts by the mercenaries who came to be known as Lorcan's dogs.

Those who rose up against the usurper – and many who didn't – were executed. The dungeon in the castle filled with the tortured and forgotten, the innocent and the damned.

Lorcan grew rich, lining his coffers with taxes, increasing his holdings with land taken by force from those who had held it, worked it, honored it for generations. He dined off plates of gold and drank his wine from goblets of crystal while the people starved.

Those who spoke against him during the dark times spoke in whispers, and in secret.

Many of the displaced took to the high hills or the Lost Forest. There magic was practiced still, and the faithful searched the sky for portents of the True One who would vanquish the snake and bring light back to the world.

There, among the farmers and merchants, the millers and artists who had become outlaws, among the faeries and elves and witches with bounties on their heads, the Travelers roamed.

'Again!' Aurora thrust with the sword and thrilled to the ring of steel against steel. She drove her opponent back, parried, pivoted.

'Balance,' Gwayne warned.

'I have my balance.' To prove it, she leapt nimbly over the sword swept at her feet, landed lightly.

Swords crossed, slid hilt to hilt. And she came up with a

dagger, pressing the point to his throat. 'And the kill,' she added. 'I like to win.'

Gwayne gave her a little poke with the dagger he held to her belly. 'So do I.'

She laughed, stepped back, then gave him a courtly bow. 'We both died well. Sit. You're winded.'

'I am not.' But he was, and he rested on a stump while she fetched a skin of water.

She has her father's eyes, he thought. Gray as woodsmoke. And her mother's soft and generous mouth. Gwynn had been right – about so many things.

The child had grown into a lithe and lovely young woman, with skin the color of pale, pure honey, hair black as midnight. A strong chin, he judged, murmuring a thanks when she offered the water. Stubborn. He hadn't known a girl-child could *be* so stubborn.

There was a light in her, so bright he wondered that those who looked on her didn't fall to their knees. She was, though garbed in hunting green and worn boots, every inch a queen.

He had done what he had been asked. She was trained in the ways of a warrior. In sword and arrow and pike, in hand against hand. She could hunt and fight and ride as well as any man he'd trained. And she could think. That was his pride in her.

Nara and Rhiann had schooled her in women's work, and in magicks. Rohan had tutored her in scholarly matters, and her mind, her thirsty mind, soaked up the songs, the stories of their people.

She could read and write, she could cipher and chart. She could make the cold fire with a thought, stitch a wound, and – these days – take him in a sword fight.

And still, how could a girl of barely twenty seasons lead her people into battle and save the world?

It haunted him at night when he lay beside Rhiann, who had become his wife. How could he honor his vow to keep her safe and honor his vow to tell her of her birthright?

'I heard the dragon in the night.'

His fingers squeezed the skin. 'What?'

'I heard it roar, in my dreams that were not dreams. The red dragon who flies in the night sky. And in his claws was a crown of stars. My wolf was with me.' She turned her head, smiled at Gwayne. 'He is always with me, it seems. So handsome and strong, with his sad eyes green as the grass on the Hills of Never.'

Even speaking of the man she thought of as her wolf had her blood warming. 'We lay on the floor of the forest and watched the sky, and when the dragon came with his crown, I felt such a thrill. Fear and wonder and joy. As I reached up, through a great wind that blew, the sky grew brighter than day, stronger than the faerie fire. And I stood beside my wolf in the blinding brightness, with blood at my feet.'

She sat on the ground, resting her back against the stump. With a careless gesture, she flipped the long, fat braid she wore behind her shoulder. 'I don't know what it means, but I wonder if I will fight for the True One. If his time draws near. I wonder if I will, at last, find the warrior who is my wolf and stand with him to lift my sword for the true king.'

She had spoken of the wolf since she could form words – the boy, and now the man, she loved. But never before had she spoken of seeing the dragon. 'Is that all the dream?'

'No.' Comfortably, she rested her head against his knee. 'In the dream that was not a dream, I saw a lady. A beautiful lady with green eyes and dark hair, and she wore the robes of royalty. She was weeping, so I said, My lady, why do you weep? She answered, I weep for the world while the world waits. It waits for the True One, I said to her, and asked, Why doesn't he come? When will he strike at Lorcan and bring peace to Twylia?'

Gwayne looked into the forest, gently stroking her hair. 'What did she say to you?'

'She said the True One's hour is midnight, in birth, in

172

death. Then she held out her hands, and in them were a globe, bright as the moon, and a star, clear as water. Take them, she told me. You will need them. Then she was gone.'

She rubbed her cheek against his knee as the sadness she'd felt came back on her. 'She was gone, Gwayne, and I ached in my heart. Beside me stood my wolf with his green eyes and dark hair. I think he was the True One, and that I'll fight for him. I think this dream was a portent, for when I woke, there was blood on the moon. A battle is coming.'

Gwynn had said he would know when it was time. He knew, sitting in the quiet forest with spring freshening the air. He knew, and it grieved him.

'Not all battles are fought and won with the sword.'

'I know. Mind and heart, vision and magic. Strategy and treachery. I feel . . .' She rose, wandered away to pluck up a stone and cast it into the silver water of the river.

'Tell me what you feel.'

She looked back. There was silver, bright as the river water, mixed with the gold of his hair, and in his beard. His eyes were a pale blue, and it seemed to her there was a shadow in them now. He was not her father. She knew her sire had fought and died in the Battle of the Stars, but Gwayne had been her father in all but blood all of her life.

There was nothing she couldn't tell him.

'I feel ... as if something inside me is waiting, as the world is waiting. I feel there is something I must do, must be beyond what I am, what I do know.' She hurried back to him, knelt at his feet. 'I feel I must find my wolf. My love for him is so great, I will never know another. If he's the one of prophecy, I want to serve him. I honor what you've given me, Gwayne. You and Rhiann, Nara and Rohan and all my family. But there's something inside me, stretching, growing restless, because it *knows*. It knows, but I can't see it.'

She rapped a fist against his leg in frustration. 'I can't see. Not yet. Not in my dreams or in the fire or the glass. When I seek, it's as if a film covers my vision and there are only shadows behind it. In the shadows I see the snake, and in the shadows my wolf is chained and bleeding.'

She rose again, impatient with herself. 'A man who might be king, a woman who was a queen. I know she was a queen, and she offered me the moon and a star. And while I wanted them with a kind of burning hunger, I feared them. Somehow, I know if I took them, everything would change.'

'I have no magic. I'm only a soldier, and it's been too long since my courage was tested. Now I taste fear, and it makes me an old man.'

'You're not old, and you're never afraid.'

'I thought there would be more time.' He got to his feet, just looked at her. 'You're so young.'

'Older than your Cyra, and she marries at the next equinox.'

'The first year of your life I thought the days would never end, and time would never pass.'

She laughed. 'Was I so troublesome an infant?'

'Restless and willful.' He reached out to touch her cheek. 'Then time flew. And here we are. Come, sit with me on the riverbank. I have many things to tell you.'

She sat with him, and watched a hawk circle in the sky. 'There is your talisman. The hawk.'

'Once, long ago, and most often behind my back, I was called the queen's hawk.'

'The queen?' Aurora looked back sharply. 'You were the queen's man? You never told me. You said you fought with my father in the great battle, but not that you were the queen's man.'

'I told you that I brought your mother out of the city, into the Lost Forest. That Rohan and the Travelers took us in, and you were born that night in the snow.'

'And she died giving me life.'

'I didn't tell you that it was she who led me, and that I left the battle with her on orders from the king. She did not want to leave him.' Though his words were spoken softly, his gaze was keen on her face. 'She fought me. She was heavy with you, but still she fought like a warrior to stay with her king. With her husband.'

'My mother.' The breath caught in her throat. 'In my dream. It was my mother.'

'It was cold, and bitter, and she was in great pain. Body and heart. But she would not stop and rest. She guided me, and we came to the camp, to the place of your birth. She wept to leave you, and held you to her breast. She charged me to keep you safe, to train you, as she charged Nara to train you. To keep the truth of your birth from you until the time had come. Then she gave you to my hands, she put you in my hands.'

He looked down at them now. 'You were born at midnight. She heard the bells, miles away in the city. Your hour is midnight. You are the True One, Aurora, and as I love you, I wish it were another.'

'How can this be?' Her heart trembled as she got to her feet, and she knew fear, the first true fear of her life. 'How can I be the one? I'm no queen, Gwayne, no ruler.'

'You are. It is your blood. From the first moment I held you in my hands, I knew this day would come. But beyond this I can see nothing.' He rose, only to kneel before her. 'I am the queen's man, and serve at your hand.'

'Don't.' Panicked, she dropped to her knees as well, gripped his shoulders. 'By Draco and all the gods, what will I do? How could I have lived all my life in comfort, never knowing true hunger or hurts while the people of the world waited? How can I stand for them, free them, when I've hidden away like a coward while Lorcan rules?'

'You were kept in safety, your mother's dying wish.' He stood, taking her arm to pull her up with him. 'You have not been a coward. Nor will you shame the memory of your mother, your father, and play the coward now. This is your fate. I have trained you as a warrior. Be a warrior.'

'I would fight.' She slapped a hand to her sword as if to prove it. 'I would pledge sword and magic, my *life*, without reserve. But to lead?' She drew a shaky breath and stared out over the river. 'Nothing is as it was only a moment ago. I need time to think.' She shut her eyes tightly. 'To breathe. I need to be alone. Give me *time*, Gwayne,' she said before he could argue. 'If you must break camp and move on, I'll find you. I need to find my way. Leave me.' She stepped aside as he reached out to touch her. 'Go.'

When she knew she was alone, she stood by the banks of the silver river and grieved for her parents, her people, and herself.

And longed for the comfort of the lover she called her wolf.

She walked deep into the forest, beyond the known and into the realm of faeries. There she cast the circle, made the fire, and sang the song for vision. She would see what had been – and what would be.

In the flames, while the moon rose and the single star that dogged it blinked to life, she saw the Battle of the Stars. She saw the bodies of servants, of children as well as soldiers. She saw the king – her father – fight like a demon, driving back the greater forces. She heard the screams, and smelled the blood.

Her father's voice came to her ears, a shouted order to Gwayne, who fought beside him, to get the queen, and the child she carried, to safety. To do this thing, as a soldier, even against the queen's orders, for the world. For the True One.

She saw her father's death, and her own birth. She tasted her mother's tears, and felt the force of love beam through the magic.

And with it, the force of duty.

'You will not shirk it.'

'Am I enough?' Aurora asked the image of her mother.

'You are the True One. There is no other. You are hope,

Aurora. And you are pride. And you are duty. You cannot turn from this.'

Aurora watched the battle, and knew it was what would come, not what had. This blood, this death, would be by her own hands. On her own hands. Even if it meant her end, she must begin. 'I have power, Mother, but it is a woman's power. Small magic. I'm strong, but I'm not seasoned. How can I lead, and rule, with so little to offer?'

'You will be more. Sleep now. Dream now.'

So she dreamed again of her wolf, her warrior with eyes as green as the hills. He was tall, and broad of shoulder. His hair, dark as her own, swept back from a face of sharp planes and angles, and a white scar slashed through his left brow like a bolt of lightning. She felt a curling in her belly that she knew for desire, one she had felt for no one but him.

'What will you be to me?' she asked him. 'What will I be to you?'

'I know only that you're my beloved. You and you alone. I've dreamed of you through my life, waking and sleeping, only of you.' He reached out, and she felt the brush of his fingers over her cheek. 'Where are you?'

'Close, I think. Close. Are you a soldier?'

He looked down at the sword in his hand, and as disgust

rippled over his face he shoved its point into the ground. 'I am nothing.'

'I think you are many things, and one of those is mine.' Giving in to curiosity, following her own will, she pulled him to her and pressed her lips to his.

The wind swirled around them, a warm wind stirred by the great beating of faerie wings. The song rose up inside her, and beat in her blood.

She would have love, she thought, even if death followed.

'I must be a woman to become what I am to become.' She stepped back, drew off her hunting tunic. 'Teach me what a woman knows. Love me in visions.'

His gaze swept down her as she stood before him, dressed only in moonbeams within the shimmering circle of magic. 'I've loved you all my life,' he said. 'And feared you.'

'I've looked for you all of mine, and come to you here, fearing everything. Will you turn from me? Will I be alone?'

'I'll never turn from you.' He drew her to him. 'I'll never leave you.'

With his lips on hers, he lowered her to the soft floor of the forest. She knew the thrill of his hands, the taste of his skin, and a pleasure, a deep and drugging pleasure that caused her body to quake. Flames leapt beside them, and inside her.

'I love you.' She murmured it as she raced her lips over his face. 'I'm not afraid.'

She rose to him, opened to him, entreated. When he joined with her, she knew the power of being a woman, and the delights.

When she woke at dawn, alone, with the fire gone to ash, she knew the cold kiss of duty.

'You should not have let her go alone.'

Gwayne sat honing his sword while Rhiann scolded and made oatcakes. The morning sounds of the camp stirred around them. Horses, dogs, women cooking at pots, children chattering, and men readying to hunt.

'It was her wish.' He spoke more sharply than he intended. 'Her command. You fret over her like a mother.'

'And what am I to her if not a mother? Two days, Gwayne, two nights.'

'If she can't stay two nights alone in the forest, she can hardly rule Twylia.'

'She's just a girl!' Rhiann slammed down her spoon. 'It was too soon to tell her of this.'

'It was time. I gave my oath on it, and it was time! Do you think I have no worries? Is there anything I would not do to keep her from harm, even to giving my life?'

She blinked back hot tears and took his hand. 'No. No. But she is like our own, as much as Cyra and young Rhys are. I want her here, sitting by the fire, putting too much honey on her oatcake, laughing. It will never be like that again.'

He set aside his sword to rise and take his wife in his arms. 'She is not ours to keep.'

Over Rhiann's head, he saw her come out of the forest, through the mists of the morning. She was tall – tall for a girl, he thought now. Straight as a soldier. She looked pale, but her eyes were clear. They met his, held.

'She is come,' Gwayne said.

Aurora heard the murmurs as she walked through camp. They had been told, she thought, and now they waited. Her family, her friends, stood beside their colorful wagons, or stepped out of them to watch her.

She stopped, waited until all was quiet. 'There is much to be done.' She lifted her voice so that it echoed through camp, and beyond. 'Eat, then come to me. I'll tell you how we will defeat Lorcan and take back our world.'

Someone cheered. She saw it was young Rhys, barely twelve, and smiled back at him. Others took up the shouts, so that she walked through the celebration of them on her way to Gwayne.

Rhys dashed to her. 'I'm not going to have to bow, am I?'

'You might, but not just now.' She ruffled his mop of golden hair.

'Good. When do we fight?'

Her stomach clutched. He was a boy, only a boy. How many boys would she send into battle? And into death? 'Soon enough.'

She stepped to Gwayne, touched Rhiann's arm to comfort her. 'I've seen the way,' she said. 'The way to begin. I'll need my hawk.'

'I'm yours.' He bowed, deep. 'Majesty.'

'Don't give me the title until I've earned it.' She sat, took an oatcake, and drenched it with honey. Beside her, Rhiann buried her face in her apron and sobbed.

'Don't weep.' Aurora rose again to gather Rhiann close. 'This is a good day.' She looked at Gwayne. 'A new day. It's not only because of what's in my blood that I can do this, but because of what you've taught me. Both of you. All of you. You've given me everything I need to meet my destiny. Rhys, will you ask Nara and Rohan to join us and break fast?'

She pressed a kiss to Rhiann's cheek as Rhys ran off. 'I've fasted for two days. I'm hungry,' she said, and with a wide grin she sat to devour her oatcakes.

3

He had known her all his life, in his mind, in his heart. She came to him first as a child, laughing as she splashed in the silver river of a deep forest.

In those days they played together, as children do. And when he knew hunger and hurt, cold and a loneliness sharper than a blade, she would comfort him.

She called him her wolf. To him she was the light.

When they were no longer children, they walked together. He knew the sound of her voice, the scent of her hair, the taste of her lips.

She was his beloved, and though he thought her only a fantasy, he clung to her for his sanity. She was the single light in a world of darkness, the only joy in a world of despair.

With her he watched the dragon roar across the sky with the crown of prophecy in its claws. Through the magic light that followed, he saw the blood stain the ground at her feet, and he felt the smooth hilt of a sword in his hand.

But he dared not hope that he would be free, at long last, to lift that sword and serve her.

He dared not hope that she was real, and that someday she would belong to him.

'Will you give me the gifts from my mother?' Aurora asked Nara.

'I've kept them for you. Rohan made this box, to keep them.' An old woman with a face scored by many seasons, Nara held out a box of polished applewood, scribed with the symbol of star and moon. It had been the royal seal of Twylia before Lorcan had ordered all such symbols out-lawed.

'It's beautiful. You honor my mother, Rohan.'

'She was a great lady.'

She opened the box and saw the clear globe, the clear star lying on dark velvet. Like the moon and star she'd seen in

185

the night sky. 'Conjured from love and grief, from joy and tears. Can there be stronger magic?'

When she lifted the globe, the light exploded in her hand. She saw through it, into the glass, into the world. Green fields sparkling in summer sunlight, wide rivers teeming with fish, thick forests where game grew fat. Cities with silver towers.

Men worked the fields, hunted the forests, fished the rivers, brought their wares to the city.

The mountains speared up, white at the peaks where the snow never melted. Beyond them, the Sea of Wonders fanned out. Other lands rose and spread. Other fields, other cities.

So they were not the world, she thought. But this was hers, to guard, to rule.

She took the star in her other hand and felt its heat, the flame of its power, fly into her.

'And the star shall burn with the blood of the dragon. Come as a lamb, mate with the wolf. Under truth is lies, under lies, truth. And valor holds its light under the coward's guise. When the witching hour comes, when the blood of the true one spills on the moon, the snake shall be vanquished, torn by the fangs of the wolf.'

She swayed, lowered the crystals in her hands. 'Who spoke?'

'You.' Gwayne's voice was thin as he stared at her. Her hair had flown out as if on a wind, and her face had been full of light, her eyes full of power. Power that struck even a warrior with edges of fear and superstition.

'I am who I was. And more. It's time to begin. To tell you, tell everyone.'

'I had visions,' Aurora said when everyone gathered around. 'Waking and dreaming. Some were shown and some were told to me, and some I know because it is my blood. I must go to the City of Stars and take my place on the throne.'

'When do we march?' Rhys shouted, and was lightly cuffed by his father.

'We will march, and we'll fight, and some of us will fall. But the world will not be freed by only the slice of a sword. It is not only might that will win what was taken from us.'

'Magic.' Rohan nodded. 'And logic.'

'Magic, logic,' Aurora agreed. 'Strategy and steel. And wiles,' she added with a sly smile. 'A woman's wiles. Cyra, what was most talked of in the village where we last stopped for supplies?'

Cyra, a blooming sixteen, still struggled not to stare at Aurora with awe. 'Prince Owen, son of Lorcan. He seeks a bride among the ranking ladies across Twylia. Orders have gone out for any knights or lords still with holdings to send their eligible daughters to the city.'

'So Owen can pick and pluck,' Aurora said with disgust. 'There will be feasting, and a grand ball, will there not, while ladies are paraded before the son of the snake like mares at auction?'

'So it's said, my . . . my lady.'

'My sister,' Aurora corrected, and made Cyra smile. 'I will go as the lamb. Can you make me look the lady, Rhiann?'

'To ride into the city unarmed—'

'I won't be unarmed.' Aurora looked at the crystals, and the sword she'd laid beside them. 'Or alone. I'll have an escort, as befits a lady of quality, and servants.' She tugged the hem of her hunting tunic. 'And a wardrobe. And so . . . garbed, I will gain access to the castle. I need men.'

Excitement rose in her. What had been stretching inside her had found its shape. She bounded onto the table, lifted her voice. 'I need men to ride out, to find the pockets of rebels, of soldiers whose swords grow dull and rusted, of their sons and daughters who would follow the True One. Find farmers willing to set aside their plows, and craftsmen willing to forge weapons for them. They must be trained, they must be forged, even as the weapons are forged, into an army. In secret, in haste.'

She looked into the forest, into the deep green of summer. 'I swear to you, before the first frost bites the air we will take the city, we will take the world, and I will have the head of the snake in my hand.'

She looked down at Gwayne. 'Will you raise my army?'

His soldier's heart thrilled. 'I will, my lady.'

'When it's time to strike, I'll send you a sign. You'll know it. Rohan, I need your maps, and your logic.'

'You'll have them.'

'Rhiann.' Aurora spread her arms. 'I need a gown.'

She was groomed and tutored, gowned and schooled. Even as Rhiann and those she deemed could run a passable seam worked on silks and velvets, Aurora practiced with sword and arrow.

She gritted her teeth as lotions were rubbed into her skin, as Cyra practiced dressing her hair. And she planned her strategy over bowls of mead, read dispatches from Gwayne, and sent them.

It was the far edge of summer when she set out, garbed in a traveling cloak of dark blue, with Cyra and Rhiann as her handmaidens and Rohan, young Rhys, and three other men as her escorts.

She would play her part, Aurora promised herself. The

gods knew she looked the pampered lady. She would charm and beguile, seduce if need be. And she would take the castle from the inside, while the army Gwayne was training came over the city walls.

It was a long journey, but she was grateful for the time. She used it to hone her vision, gather her courage, strengthen her purpose.

The fields were still green, she noted, whoever ruled. But she'd seen the fear, the distrust, and the anger in the eyes of men they passed on the road. She'd seen the crows picking at the bones of those who had been unlucky enough to be set upon by thieves, or Lorcan's dogs.

Children, their faces pinched with hunger, begged for food or coin. She saw what was left of homes that had been burned to the ground, and the desperate eyes of women with no man left to protect them.

Had she not looked so closely before? Aurora wondered. Had she been so content to run through the forest, to sing in the hills, that she hadn't seen the utter despair of her people, the waste of her land?

She would give her life to put it right again.

'It seems so strange to see Grandfather garbed so richly,' Cyra said.

'You must not call him Grandfather.'

'No, I'll remember. Are you afraid, Aurora?'

'I am. But it's a good fear. The kind that tells me something will happen.'

'You look beautiful.'

Aurora smiled, and struggled not to tug at the confining gown. 'It's only another weapon, and one I find I don't mind wielding. A sprinkle of witchcraft and . . . he'll look on me, won't he, this son of a demon? He'll look on me and want?'

'Any man would.'

Satisfied, Aurora nodded. While he looked, and wanted, she would seek another. She would seek her wolf.

He was there. Waiting. She felt him in her blood, and with every league they traveled, that blood warmed.

She would find her love, at last, in the City of Stars.

And her destiny.

'Oh, look!' Cyra bounced in her seat. 'The city. See how the towers shine.'

Aurora saw it, in the distance, the silver and gilt that spread up into the sky. The grand towers of the castle gleamed, and on the topmost, the black flag with its coiled red snake flew.

She would burn it, she vowed. Burn it to ash and hoist her family crest in its place. The gold dragon on its white field would fly again.

'Twenty men on the castle walls,' Rohan said quietly as he rode his mount sedately toward her.

'Yes, I see them. And more at the city gates. He will have a personal guard as well, others at the castle gates. Some will slip away once Lorcan is dead, some will certainly join our cause. But others will fight. We'll need to know the castle, every foot of it. Gwayne's drawings are a start, but it's likely Lorcan has changed some of it over the years.'

'On the sweat and blood of the people,' Rohan agreed. 'Building fine rooms and thicker walls.' He had to remind himself not to spit. 'However fine the gilt, he's turned the City of Stars into the pit of a snake.'

'And I will bury him in it.'

She fixed a bored expression on her face, and watched everything, as they rode through the gates of the city.

In the stables, Thane groomed the roan mare. He worked alone, and the work was endless. But he was used to that, to the aching muscles, the weary bones at the end of the day.

And he had come to prize his solitude.

He loved the horses. That was his secret. If Owen and Lorcan knew he enjoyed them, they would cast him out of the stables and the dim quiet that brought him some measure, at least, of peace. They would find him other drudgery, he thought. It pleased them to do so. He was used to that as well.

He'd learned as a very young boy to keep his words and his opinions to himself, to do his work, expect nothing — unless it was the heel of a boot in the ass. As long as he controlled his temper, his fury, his hatred, he had the gift of alone.

And those he loved were safe.

The mare blew softly as he ran a hand over her silky neck. For a moment, Thane laid his cheek to hers, shut his eyes. He was exhausted. Dreams plagued him, night after night, so that he woke hot and hard and needy. Voices and visions ran through his head and gave him no answers, and no relief.

Even his light, his love, brought a strange restlessness to him.

He could not war, could not find peace, so there seemed nothing for him but hours of work.

He stepped away from the mare, ran a hand through his unruly black hair. He would have gone to the next mount, but something stirred in his belly, a kind of hunger that had nothing to do with desire for food.

He felt his heart thudding in his chest as he walked past the stalls, toward the stable entrance, where the light fell like a curtain of gold.

He lifted his hand to shield his eyes from the glare and saw her, his vision, mounted on a white stallion. Blood roared into his head, made him giddy as he stared.

She was smiling, her lashes downcast. And he knew – he *knew* the eyes they hid were gray as smoke. Dimly, he heard her voice, heard her laugh – how well he knew that voice, that laugh – as she offered Owen her hand.

'Servants will see to your horses, my lady . . .'

'I am Aurora, daughter of Ute of the westland. My father sends his regrets for not accompanying me to honor you, Prince Owen. He is unwell.'

'He is forgiven for sending such a jewel.'

She did her best to work up a flush, and fluttered her lashes. He was handsome, with the look of a young, golden god. Unless you looked in his eyes, as she did. There was the snake. He was his father's son.

'You flatter me, sir, and I thank you. I must beg your indulgence. My horses are precious to me, I fear I fret over them like a hen over chicks. I'd like to see the stables, if you please, and speak with the grooms about their care.'

'Of course.' He put his hands around her waist. She didn't stiffen as she wished to, but smiled prettily as he lifted her down.

'The city is magnificent.' She brushed a hand over her headdress as if to fuss it into place. 'A country lass like myself is awed by so much' – she looked back at him now deliberately provocative – 'glamour.'

'It dulls before you, Lady Aurora.' Then he turned, and she saw his handsome face go hard with temper and those dark eyes gleam with hate.

She followed his glance and felt her world tilt.

She had found her wolf. He was dressed in rags, with the sweat of labor staining them. His dark hair curled madly around a face smudged with stable dirt. And in his hand he carried not a sword but a currycomb.

Their eyes met, and in that single instant she felt the shock of knowledge, and of disbelief.

He took one step toward her, like a man in a trance.

In three strides, Owen stormed to Thane and used the back of his hand to deliver a vicious blow that drew blood. For an instant, only an instant, rage flamed in Thane's eyes. Then he lowered them, as Owen struck again.

'On your knees, worthless cur. You dare cast your eyes on a lady. You'll be whipped for this insult.'

Head down, Thane lowered to his knees. 'Your pardon, my lord prince.'

'If you have time to stand and stare at your betters, you must not have enough to do.' Owen pulled out his riding crop, raised it.

To Aurora's disappointment, the wolf of her visions stayed down like a cowed dog.

'Prince Owen.' Her knees shook, and her heart thundered. Every instinct had to be denied. She couldn't go to him, speak to him. She must instead play the pampered lady. However it scored her pride, Aurora laid the back of her hand on her brow and pretended to swoon. 'I can't bear violence,' she said weakly when he rushed back to catch her. 'I feel . . . unwell.'

'Lady, I'm sorry you had to witness such a . . . display.' He looked down on Thane with derision. 'This stableboy has some skill with horses, but too often forgets his place.'

'Please, don't punish him on my account. I couldn't bear the thought of it.' She waved a hand, and after a moment's confusion, Cyra rushed forward with a bottle of salts to hold under Aurora's nose.

'Enough, enough.' Aurora nudged her away as the salts made her eyes water. 'If you could assist me, my lord, out of the sun?'

'Forgive me, Lady Aurora. Let me take you inside, offer you some refreshment.'

'Oh, yes.' She leaned against him. 'Traveling is so wearing, isn't it?'

She let him lead her away from the stables. Her heart was

heavy to find her wolf, at last, and learn he had neither fang nor claw.

Feigning light-headedness, she let herself be led across a courtyard and into the keep. And she noted every detail. The number of guards and their weapons, the richness of the tapestries and tiles, the placement of windows and doors and stairs.

She noted the stone faces and downcast eyes of servants, and the demeanor of the other women, other ladies brought in like broodmares for display.

Some, it seemed to her, were pleased to be considered worthy of Prince Owen's regard. In others, she saw fear lurking in the eyes.

Women were chattel under Lorcan's reign. Property to be owned by father, husband, brother, or any man with the price. Any suspected of witchcraft were burned.

Women were lesser creatures, Rohan had told her, in Lorcan's world. All the better, she thought. He would hardly suspect that the True One was a woman, and that she bided under his roof until she could slit his throat.

She fluttered and flushed and begged Owen that she be taken to her chambers to rest away the fatigue of the journey.

When she had safely arrived there, she balled her hands

into fists. 'Simpleton. Bully. Bastard.' She took a deep breath and fought for control. 'Calling him prince makes my tongue ache.'

'He was cruel to that boy,' Rhiann murmured.

'It wasn't a boy, but a man. A man without a backbone.' With a hiss of rage, she dropped into a chair. The man of her dreams would not grovel in the dirt. She would *not* love a man who would beg pardon of an ass.

So she would forget him. She had to forget him and her woman's heart, and do what came next.

'We're inside,' she said to Rhiann. 'I'll write a dispatch to Gwayne. See that it's sent today.'

4

Aurora dressed with great care in a gown of blue velvet piped with gold. With Cyra's help her heavy hair was tamed into a gold snood. She wore small blue stones at her ears, a delicate pearl cross at her throat. And a dagger strapped to her thigh.

After practicing her smiles and simpers in the glass, she deemed herself ready. She wandered the gallery, knowing that the art and furnishings there had been stolen from her parents or looted from other provinces. She gazed out the windows at the gardens and mazes and lands that had been tended by her forebears, then taken by force for another's pride and greed.

And she noted the numbers and locations of guards at every post. She swept down the stairs, meandered into rooms, watched the servants and guests and courtiers.

It pleased her to be able to move freely through the castle, around the gardens. What threat was a woman after all, she thought as she stopped to smell the golden roses and study the rank of guards along the seawall. She was simply a candidate for Owen's hand, sent to offer herself like a ripe fruit for the plucking.

'Where is the music?' she asked Cyra. 'Where is the laughter? There are no songs in Lorcan's kingdom, no joy. He rules shadows.'

'You will bring back the light.'

'I swear that I will.' Or die in the attempt, she vowed silently. 'There's such beauty here, but it's like beauty trapped behind a locked glass. Imprisoned, waiting. We must shatter the glass.'

She rounded a bend in the path and saw a woman seated on a bench with a young girl kneeling at her feet, weeping. The woman wore a small crown atop her golden hair. She looked brittle and thin in her rich robes, and though her face held beauty, it was pale and tired.

'She who calls herself queen.' Aurora spoke softly and fought to keep the fury out of her eyes. 'Lorcan's wife, who was my mother's woman. There's time before the banquet. We'll see if she can be of use.'

Folding her hands at her waist, Aurora stepped forward. She saw the queen start, saw her hand close tight over the girl's shoulder. 'Majesty.' Aurora dropped into a deep curtsy. 'I am Lady Aurora, and beg pardon for disturbing you. May I help?'

The girl had shut off her tears, and though her pretty face was ravaged by them, she got to her feet, bowed. 'You are welcome, lady. You will excuse my behavior. It was only a childish trifle that had me seeking my mother's knee. I am Dira, and I welcome you to the City of Stars and our home.'

'Highness.' Aurora curtsied, then took the hand the queen offered.

'I am Brynn. I hope you have all that you require here.'

'Yes, my lady. I thought to walk the gardens before the sun set. They are so lovely, and with summer nearly done, transient.'

'It grows cold at twilight.' Brynn gathered her cloak at her throat as if she could already feel the oncoming winter. When Brynn rose, Aurora noted that her eyes were strongly blue, and unbearably sad. 'Will you accompany us inside? It's nearly time for feasting.'

'With pleasure, my lady. We live quiet in the west,' she continued. 'I look forward to the dancing and feasting, and the time with other women.'

'Partridges and peahens,' Dira whispered.

'Dira!'

But Aurora laughed over the queen's sharp rebuke, and glanced at the girl with more interest. 'So we must seem to you, Highness. Country girls parading in their finery with hopes that Prince Owen will show favor.'

'I meant no offense.'

'And none was given. It must be wearying to have so much female chattering about day and night. You'll be happy, I'm sure, when the prince has chosen his bride. Then you will have a sister, will you not?'

Dira looked away, toward the seawall. 'So it would seem.'

A shadow crossed the path, and Aurora would have sworn the world went still.

Lorcan, self-proclaimed king of Twylia, stood before them.

He was tall and strongly built. His hair, nearly copper in color, spilled to the shoulders of his purple cloak. Jewels glinted in his crown, on his fingers. His sharply ridged face had the devil's own beauty, and so cold was the blue of his eyes that Aurora wasn't surprised to feel the queen tremble beside her.

'You dally in the garden while our guests wait? You sit and dream when you are commanded to take your place?'

'Your Majesty.' Going with instinct, Aurora lowered herself to one knee at the king's feet, and used a small dash of power to draw his attention and thought to her and away from his wife. 'I most humbly beg your pardon for detaining Queen Brynn with my witless chatter. Her Majesty was too kind to send me away and she sought to soothe my foolish nerves. I am to blame for the lateness of her arrival.' She looked up and put what she hoped was the slightest light of flirtation in her eyes. 'I was nervous, sire, to meet the king.'

It was, she realized as his taut mouth relaxed, the right touch. He reached down, lifted her chin. 'And who is this dark flower?'

'Sire, I am Aurora, daughter of Ute, and the foolish woman who has earned your displeasure.'

'They grow them fair in the west. Rise.' He drew her to her feet and studied her face so boldly she didn't have to fake a blush. Though it came more from temper than modesty. 'You will sit beside me at tonight's banquet.'

Luck or fate had blessed her, Aurora thought, and laid her hand on his. 'I am undeserving, and grateful for the honor, sire.'

'You will entertain me,' he said as he led her inside, without, Aurora noted, another glance at his wife or daughter. 'And perhaps show me why my son should consider you for wife.'

'The prince should consider me, sire, so that I might continue to entertain you, and serve you as a daughter would, all of your days.'

He glanced back at Dira now, with thinly veiled disgust. 'And how might a daughter serve me?'

'To do her duty. At the king's pleasure, sire, and at her husband's. To bear strong sons and to present a pleasing face and form. To do their bidding day and . . . night.'

He laughed, and when he stepped inside the crowded and brightly lit banquet hall, Aurora was at his side.

Thane watched from the spy hole in the secret chamber beside the minstrel's gallery. From there he could look down on the feasting, and the lights and the colors. At the scent of roasted meat his empty belly clutched, but he was used to hunger. Just as he was used to standing in the shadows and looking out on the color and the light.

He could hear women's laughter as the ladies vied for Owen's attention and favor, but there was only one who drew Thane's interest.

She sat beside the king, smiling, sampling the delicacies he piled on her plate, flirting with her eyes over the rim of her goblet.

How could this be the same creature who had come to him in dream and vision the whole of his life? The woman who had offered him such love, such passion, and such shining honesty? This coy miss with her sly smiles and trilling laugh could never make him burn as her light made him burn.

Yet he burned, even now, just watching her.

'Your back needs tending.'

Thane didn't turn. Kern appeared when and where he chose, as faeries were wont to do. And was as much bane as blessing.

'I've been whipped before. It'll heal soon enough.'

'Your flesh may.' Kern waved a hand and the wall between them and the banquet hall shimmered away. 'But your heart is another matter. She is very beautiful.'

'A fair face is easy beauty. She isn't what I thought she was ... would be. I don't want her.'

Kern smiled. 'One doesn't always want destiny.'

Thane turned. Kern was old, old as time. His long gray beard covered plump cheeks and spun down to the waist of his bright red robes. But his eyes were merry as a child's, and green as the Lost Forest.

'You show me these things. This woman, this world, and you hint of changes, of restoration.' Frustration edged Thane's voice and hardened his face. 'You train me for battle, and you heal my hurts when Owen or Lorcan or one of their dogs beats me. But what good does it do me? My mother, my young sister, are no more than prisoners still. And Leia—'

'She is safe. Have I not told you?'

'Safe, at least.' Struggling to compose himself, Thane looked back at the feasting, at little Dira. 'One sister safe, and lost to me, the other trapped here until she's old enough for me to find sanctuary for her. There will never be one for my mother. She grows so thin.'

'She worries for you, for her daughters.'

'Leia bides with the women in the Valley of Secrets, at least for now. And Dira is yet too young for the snake to pay her mind – or to plan to marry her off to some slathering lackey. She need not worry for them. She need not think of me at all. I am nothing but a coward who hides his sword.'

'It's not cowardice to hide your sword until the time comes to wield it. The time draws near.'

'So you always say,' Thane replied, and though he knew that Kern's magick kept those who were feasting from seeing him above them, he felt Aurora's gaze as it scanned the gallery. He knew she looked at him, just as he looked at her. 'Is she a witch, then, and the visions between us an amusement to her?'

'She is many things.'

Thane shook his head. 'It doesn't matter. She isn't for me, nor I for her. That was fantasy and foolishness, and is done. It's Dira who concerns me now. Another two years, then Lorcan will seek to marry her off. Then she must be sent away from here, for her own safety. My mother will have no daughter to comfort her, and no son to stand for her.'

'You are no good to them dead.' Kern's voice went sharp as honed steel. 'And no good to any when you wallow in pity.'

'Easily said when your time is spent in a raft, and mine in a stable. I gave up my pride, Kern, and have lived without it since my seventh season. Is it so surprising I should be ready to give up my hope?'

'If you do, it will be the end for you.'

'There are times I'd welcome the end.' But he looked at

Dira. She was so young. Innocent and defenseless. He thought of how she had wept to find him beaten and bleeding in the stables. It hurt her, he knew, more than the lash hurt him. Lorcan's blood might have run through her, but she had none of his cruelty.

She was, he thought, his only real pleasure since Leia's escape. So he would hold on to his hope a while longer, for her.

'I don't give up yet,' Thane said quietly. 'Not yet. But it had best be soon.'

'Come, then, let me tend your wounds.'

'No.' Thane rolled his shoulders, welcomed the pain. 'It reminds me. I have work.'

'When it's done, meet me. It's time to practice.'

Fingertip to fingertip, Aurora circled with Owen in a dance. The music was lively, and pleased her a great deal more than her partner. But he couldn't have known of her displeasure as she smiled at him and sent him a laughing glance over her shoulder when the set parted them.

When the music brought them together again, he stroked his thumb over her knuckles. 'The king has favored you.'

'I am honored. I see much of him in you, my lord.'

'When it's my time to rule, I will outreach him.' His

fingers squeezed hers. 'And I will demand much more of my queen than he of his.'

'And what does your father demand of his queen?'

'Little more than obedience.' He looked over to where Brynn sat, like a statue, with her women. 'A comely face, a bowed head, and two pale daughters will not be enough for me.'

'Two?'

'Dira is the youngest of Brynn's whelps. There was another, but she was killed by wild beasts in the Black Forest.'

'Wild beasts!' Though she couldn't manage a squeal, Aurora clasped a hand to her breast.

'Do not fear, my lady.' He smirked. 'There are no beasts in the city – none that walk on four legs.'

The figures of the dance parted them again, and Aurora executed her turns, her curtsies, and counted the beats impatiently until she faced Owen once more. With her head saucily angled, she stared into his eyes. 'And what would be enough for you, my lord, for a queen?'

'Passion. Fire. Sons.'

'There must be fire in bed to get sons.' She lowered her voice, and spoke with her face close to his. 'I would burn to be the mother of kings.'

Then she stepped back, dipped low as the dance ended. 'Walk with me.'

'With pleasure, sir. But I must have my woman with me, as is proper.'

'Do you do only what is proper?'

'A queen would, when eyes are on her.'

He lifted a brow in approval. 'A brain as well as beauty. Bring her, then.'

Aurora put her hand in his and gestured carelessly with the other so Cyra followed them out onto the terrace. 'I like the sea,' she began, looking out over the cliffs. 'The sounds and the smells of it. It's a wall to the back, protection from enemies. But it's also passion, and possibilities. Do you believe there are worlds beyond the world, my lord prince?'

'Tales for children.'

'If there were, a king could rule them all, and the sons of such a king would be gods. Even Draco would bow.'

'Draco's power is weak, so he sulks in his cave. This' – Owen laid a hand on the hilt of his sword – 'this is power.'

'A man's power is in his sword and arm, a woman's is in her mind and womb.'

'And her heart?' Now he laid a hand on her breast.

Though her skin crawled, she smiled easily. 'Not if she gives that heart away.' She touched her fingers lightly to his wrist, then eased away. 'If I were to do so, my lord, to offer you my heart and my body, my value to you would diminish. A prize easily taken is little prize at all. So I will bid you good night, and hope you consider what I hold to be worth the winning.'

'You would leave me with so many choices?' He gestured toward the women in the banquet hall as Aurora moved away.

'So you will see them . . . but think of me.' She left him with a laugh, then turned to a mumbled oath when she was certain she was out of earshot.

'Empty-headed, fat-fingered *toad*! He's a man who thinks first with the lance between his legs. Well, there is little warrior in him. I've learned that much at least. Cyra, I need you to talk with the other women, find out all you can about the queen and her daughters. What are they in this puzzle?'

She cut herself off as they walked past guards and began to talk brightly of the feasting and dancing until she was back in her chambers.

'Rhiann.' She let out a huge sigh. 'Help me out of this gown. How do women of court bear the weight every day? I need the black tunic.'

'You're going out again?'

'Yes. I felt eyes on me when I was at banquet. Eyes from

above. Gwayne said there was a spy hole next to the minstrel's gallery. I want a look. Would Lorcan station guards
there during a feast? He seems too sure of himself to bother.'

No, it had not been guards watching her, Aurora knew.
It had been the grass-green eyes of her wolf. She needed to
learn why he'd been there.

'And I need to see how the castle is protected during the
night.' She pulled on her tunic. 'I have enough magic to go
unnoticed if need be. Did you learn anything of use?' she
asked as she strapped on her sword.

'I learned that Owen went back and beat the stable hand
after all.'

Aurora's mouth tightened. 'I'm sorry for it.'

'And that the stable hand is Thane, son of Brynn, whom
Lorcan took as queen.'

Aurora's hands paused in the act of braiding her hair, and
her eyes met Rhiann's in the glass. 'Brynn's son is cast to the
stables? And remains there? His father was a warrior who died
in battle beside mine. His mother was my own mother's hand-
maid. Yet their son grovels at Owen's feet and grooms horses.'

'He was not yet four when Lorcan took the throne. Only
a child.'

'He is not a child today.' She swirled on her cloak, drew
up the hood. 'Stay inside,' she ordered.

She slipped out of the chamber, moved silently down the corridors toward the stairs. She drew on her magic to bring smoke into the air, blunt the guards' senses as she hurried by them.

She dashed up to the minstrel's gallery and found the mechanism Gwayne had described for her to open the secret room beside it. Once inside, she approached the spy hole and looked down at the hall.

It was nearly empty now, and servants were beginning to clear the remnants of the feast. The queen had retired, and all but the boldest ladies had followed suit. The laughter had taken on a raucous edge. She saw one of the courtiers slide his hand under the bodice of a woman's gown and fondle her breast.

She hadn't been sheltered from the ways of men and women. The Travelers could be earthy, but there was always a respect and good nature. This, she thought, had neither.

She turned away from it, and focused instead on the essence of what had been in the room before her.

One that was human, she thought, and one that was not. Man and faerie-folk. But what had been their purpose?

To find out, she followed the trail of that essence from the room and out of the castle. Into the night.

There were guards posted on walls, at the gates, but to

Aurora's eyes they looked sleepy and dull. Even two hundred good men, she calculated, could take the castle if it was done swiftly and with help from inside. As she worked her way along the wall, she heard the snores of a guard sleeping on duty.

Lorcan, she thought, took much for granted.

She looked toward the south gate. It was there that Gwayne had fled with the queen on the night of the battle. Many brave men had lost their lives so that her mother could escape, so that she could be born.

She would not forget it. And she would take nothing for granted.

Her senses drew her toward the stables. She smelled the horses, heard them shifting in their stalls as she approached. Though she scented man as well – sweat and blood – she knew she wouldn't find him there.

She stopped to stroke her horse's nose, to inspect the stall, and others. Whatever Thane was, he did his job here well. And lived poorly, she noted as she studied the tiny room that held his bedding, the stub of a candle, and a trunk of rough clothes.

Following the diagram in her mind, she searched the floor for the trapdoor that led to the tunnels below the stables. One channel ran to the sea, she remembered, the other to the forest.

It would be a good route to bring in her soldiers, to have

them take the castle from the inside. If Lorcan hadn't found it and destroyed it.

But when she opened the door, she felt the air stir. Taking the candle stub, she lit the wick and let its wavery light guide her down the rough steps.

She could hear the roar of the sea, and though she was tempted to take that channel, just to stand by the water, to breathe it in, she turned toward the second path.

She would have Gwayne bring the men through the forest, split into companies. Some to take the walls, others to take the tunnels. Attack the walls first, she calculated, drawing Lorcan's forces there while the second wave came in from under – and behind.

Before he could turn and brace for the second assault, they would run him over. And it would be done.

She prayed that it could be done, and that she would not be sending good men to their deaths for nothing.

She moved slowly through the dark. The low ceiling made it impossible to stand upright, and she could imagine the strain of a man making the same trek in full armor.

And it would be done not after a night of feasting and dancing but after a hard march from the hills, through the forest, with the knowledge that death could wait at the end of the journey.

She was asking this of her people, and asking that they trust the fates that she would be worthy of their sacrifice. That she would be a worthy queen.

She stopped, bracing her back against the wall of stone and dirt as her heart ached. She would wish with every ounce of her blood that it was not so. That she was only an ordinary woman and could leap onto her horse and ride with the Travelers again, as she had always done. She would wish that she could hunt and laugh, love a man and bear his children. Live a life that she understood.

But to wish it was to wish against the fates, to diminish the sacrifices her parents had made, and to turn her back on those who prayed for the True One to come and bring them back into light.

So she lifted her candle again and headed down the tunnel to plot out her strategy.

When she heard the clash of steel, she drew her own sword. Snuffing out the candle, she set it down and moved soft as a cat toward the narrow opening.

She could see them battling in the moonlight, the young man and the old. And neither noticed as she boosted herself out of the tunnel and crouched on the floor of the forest.

5

Here was her wolf, and she thrilled to see him.

He fought with an icy focus and relentless strength that Aurora admired and respected – and envied. The skill, yes, the skill of a warrior was there, but it was enhanced by that coldblooded, cold-eyed style that told her he would accept death or mete it out with equal dispatch.

The faerie was old, it was true, but a faerie nonetheless. Such creatures were not vanquished easily.

She could see the sweat of effort gleaming on Thane's

face, and how it dampened his shirt. And she saw the blood that seeped onto the cloth from the wounds on his back, still fresh from a lashing.

How could a man wield a sword with such great talent and allow himself to be flogged?

And why had he watched the feasting through the spy hole? It was his gaze she had sensed on her. And his essence she had sensed there. His, and that of the old graybeard he battled now.

Even as she puzzled it over, two columns of smoke spiraled on either side of Thane. And became armed warriors. He blocked the sword of the one on his right and spun away from the sword of the one on his left as it whizzed through the air.

Raising her own, Aurora leapt. She cleaved her blade through one of the warriors and vanished it back to smoke. 'Foul play, old one.' She pivoted, and would have struck Kern down if Thane hadn't crossed swords with her.

'At your back,' she snapped out, but the warrior was smoke again with a wave of Kern's hand.

'Lady,' the faerie said with an undeniable chuckle, 'you mistake us. I only help my young friend with his training.' To prove it, Kern lowered his sword and bowed.

'Why am I dreaming?' Thane demanded. He was out of

breath as he hadn't been during the bout, and the surging of his blood had nothing to do with swordplay. 'What test is this?'

'You are not dreaming,' Kern assured him.

'She's not real. I've seen her now, in flesh. And this is the vision, not the woman.' Love, lust, longing knotted inside him so that he fought to ice his words with annoyance. 'And neither holds interest for me any longer.'

'I'm as real as you,' Aurora tossed back, then sheathing her sword, she twisted her lips into a sneer. 'You fight well. For a groveling stableboy. And your sword would be all that interests me, if I believed you'd gather the courage and wit to use it on something more than smoke.'

'So, no vision, then, but the simpering, swooning female.' He lifted the cape she'd tossed aside when she leapt to his defense. With a mocking bow, he held it out. 'Go back to your feather bed, else you catch a chill.'

'I'm chilled enough from you.' She knocked his hand aside and turned on Kern. 'Why haven't you treated his wounds?'

'He doesn't wish it.'

'Ah, he's stupid, then.' She inclined her head toward Thane again. 'Whether you are stupid or not, I regret you were beaten on my account.'

'It's nothing to do with you.' Because the beating still shamed him, he rammed his sword back into its sheath. 'It's not safe for a woman alone beyond the walls. Kern will show you the way back.'

'I found my way out, I can find my way back. I'm not some helpless female,' she said impatiently. 'You of all men should know—'

'I do not know you,' Thane said dully.

She absorbed the blow to her heart. They stood in the dappled moonlight, with only the call of an owl and the rushing of a stream over rocks to break the silence between them.

Even knowing the risk of mediation, Kern stepped up, laying a hand on Thane's shoulder, the other on Aurora's. 'Children,' he began brightly.

'We're not children any longer. Are we, lady? Not children splashing in rivers, running through the forest.' It scored his heart to remember it, to remember the joy and pleasure, the simple comfort of those times with her. To know they were ended forever. 'Not children taking innocent pleasure in each other's company.'

She shook her head, and thought how she had lain with him, in love, in visions. Him and no other. 'I wonder,' she said after a moment, 'why we need to hurt each other this way. Why we strike out where we once – where we always reached out. And I fear you're right. You don't know me, nor I you. But I know you're the son of a warrior, you have noble blood. Why do you sleep in the stables?'

'Why do you smile at Lorcan, dance with Owen, then wander the night with a sword?'

She only smiled. 'It's not safe for a woman alone beyond the walls.' There was, for just an instant, a glint of humor in his eyes. 'You watched me dance.'

He cursed himself for speaking of it. Now she knew of the spy hole as well as the tunnels. And one word to Owen ... 'If you wish to make amends for the beating, you won't speak of seeing me here.'

'I have no reason to speak of you at all,' she said coolly. 'I was told faeries no longer bided near the city.'

At her comment Kern shrugged. 'We bide where we will, lady, even under Lorcan's reign. Here is my place, and he is my charge.'

'I am no one's charge. Are you a witch?' Thane demanded.

'A witch is one of what I am.' He looked so angry and frustrated. How she longed to stroke her finger over the lightning-bolt scar above his eye. 'Do you fear witchcraft, Thane of the stables?'

Those eyes fired at the insult, as she'd hoped. 'I don't fear you.'

'Why should an armed man and his faerie guard fear a lone witch?'

'Leave us,' Thane demanded of Kern, and his gaze stayed locked on Aurora's face.

'As you wish.' Kern bowed deeply, then disappeared.

'Why are you here?'

'Prince Owen needs a wife. Why shouldn't it be me?'

He had to choke down a rage, bubbling black, at the thought of it. 'Whatever you are, you're not like the others.'

'Why? Because I walk alone at night in the Black Forest, where wild beasts are said to roam?'

'You're not like the others. I know you. I do know you, or what you were once.' He had to curl his hand into a fist to keep from touching her. 'I've seen you in my dreams. I've tasted your mouth. I'll taste it again.'

'In your dreams perhaps you will. But I don't give my kisses to cowards who fight only smoke.'

She turned, and was both surprised and aroused when he gripped her arm and dragged her around. 'I'll taste it again,' he repeated.

Even as he yanked her close, she had the point of her dagger at his throat. 'You're slow.' She all but purred it.

'Release me. I don't wish to slit your throat for so small an offense.'

He eased back and, when she lowered the dagger, moved like lightning. He wrested the dagger from her hand, kicked her feet out from under her before she could draw her sword. The force of the fall knocked the wind out of her, and she was pinned under him before she could draw a breath.

'You're rash,' he told her, 'to trust an enemy.'

She had to swallow the joy, and the laugh. They'd wrestled like this before, when there had been only love and innocence between them. Here was her man, after all.

'You're right. The likes of you would have no honor.'

With the same cold look in his eyes that she'd seen when he fought, he dragged her arms over her head. She felt the first licks of real fear, but even that she held tight. No groveling stableboy could make her fear. 'I will taste you again. I will take something. There has to be something.'

She didn't struggle. He'd wanted her to, wanted her to spit and buck and fight him so he wouldn't have to think. For one blessed moment, not to think but only feel. But she went still as stone when he crushed his lips to hers.

Her taste was the same, the same as he'd imagined, remembered, wished. Hot and strong and sweet. So he couldn't think, after all, but simply sank into the blessed relief of her. And all the aches and misery, the rage and the despair, washed out of him in the flood of her.

She didn't fight him, as she knew she wouldn't win with force. She remained still, knowing that a man wanted response – heat, anger or acquiescence, but not indifference.

She didn't fight him, but she began to fight herself as his mouth stirred her needs, as the weight of his body on hers brought back wisps of memories.

She'd never really been with a man, but only with him in visions, in dreams. She had wanted no man but him, for the whole of her life. But what she'd found wasn't the wolf she'd known, nor the coward she thought she'd found. It was a bitter and haunted man.

Still, her heart thundered, her skin trembled, and beneath his, her mouth opened and offered. She heard him speak, one word, in the oldest tongue of Twylia. The desperation in his voice, the pain and the longing in it made her heart weep.

The word was 'Beloved.'

He eased up to look at her. There was a tear on her cheek, and more in her eyes where the moonlight struck them. He closed his own eyes and rolled onto his bloody back.

'I've lived with horses too long, and forget how to be a man.'

She was shaken to the bone from her feelings, from her needs, from the loss. 'Yes, you forget to be a man.' As she had forgotten to be a queen. 'But we'll blame this on the night, on the strangeness of it.' She got to her feet, walked over to pick up her dagger. 'I think perhaps this is some sort of test, for both of us. I've loved you as long as I remember.'

He looked at her, into her, and for one moment that was all there was, the love between them. It shimmered, wide and deep as the Sea of Wonders. But in the next moment the heavy hand of duty took over.

'If things were different . . .' Her vision blurred – not with magicks but with a woman's tears. It was the queen who forced them back, and denied herself the comfort. 'But they aren't, and this can't be between us, Thane, for there's more at stake. Yet I have such longing for you, as I have always. Whatever's changed, that never will.'

'We're not what we were in visions, Aurora. Don't seek me in them, for I won't come to you. We live as we live in the world.'

She crouched beside him, brushed the hair from his brow. 'Why won't you fight? You have a warrior's skill. You could leave this place, join the rebels and make something of yourself. Why raise a pitchfork in the stables when you can raise a sword against an enemy? I see more in you than what they've made you.'

And want more of you, she thought. So much more of you.

'You speak of treason.' His voice was colorless in the dark.

'I speak of hope, of right. Have you no beliefs in the world, Thane? None of yourself?'

'I do what I'm fated to do. No more, no less.' He moved away from her and sat, staring into the thick shadows. 'You should not be here, my lady. Owen would never select a wife bold enough to roam the forest alone, or one who would permit a stable hand to take ... liberties.'

'And if he selects me, what will you do?'

'Do you taunt me?' He sprang to his feet, and she saw what she'd hoped to see in his face. The strength and the fury. 'Does it amuse you to find that I could pine for one who would offer herself to another like a sweetmeat on a platter?'

'If you were a man, you would take me – then it would be done.' If you would take me, she thought, perhaps things would be different after all.

'Simply said when you have nothing to lose.'

'Is your life so precious you won't risk it to take what belongs to you? To stand for yourself and your world?'

He looked at her, the beauty of her face and the purpose that lit it like a hundred candles glowing from within her. 'Yes, life is precious. Precious enough that I would debase myself day after day to preserve it. Your place isn't here. Go back before you're missed.'

'I'll go, but this isn't done.' She reached out, touched his cheek. 'You needn't worry. I won't tell Owen or Lorcan about the tunnels or the spy hole. I'll do nothing to take away your small pleasures or to bring you harm. I swear it.'

His face went to stone as he stepped back, and he executed a mocking little bow. 'Thank you, my lady, for your indulgence.'

Her head snapped back as if he'd slapped her. 'It's all I can give you.' She hurried back to the tunnel and left him alone.

She slept poorly and watched the dawn rise in mists. In that half-light, Aurora took the globe out of its box, held it in the palm of her hand.

'Show me,' she ordered, and waited while the sphere shimmered with colors, with shapes.

She saw the ballroom filled with people, heard the music and the gaiety of a masque. Lorcan slithered among the guests, a serpent in royal robes with his son and heir

227

strutting in his wake. The black wolf prowled among them like a tame dog. Though his eyes were green and fierce, he kept his head lowered and kept to heel. Aurora saw the thick and bloody collar that choked his neck.

She saw Brynn chained to the throne with her daughter bound at her feet, and the ghost of another girl weeping behind a wall of glass.

And through the sounds of lutes and harps she heard the calls and cries of the people shut outside the castle. Pleas for mercy, for food, for salvation.

She was robed in regal red. the sword she raised shot hot white light from its killing point. As she whirled toward Lorcan, bent on vengeance, the world erupted. The battle raged – the clash of steel, the screams of the dying. She heard the hawk cry as an arrow pierced its heart. The dragon folded its black wings and sank into a pool of blood.

Flames sprang up at her feet, ate up her body until she was a pillar of fire.

And while she burned, Lorcan smiled, and the black wolf licked his hand.

Failure and death, she thought as the globe went black as pitch in her hand. Had she come all this way to be told her sword would not stand against Lorcan? Her friends would die, the battle would be lost, and she would be burned as a witch while Lorcan continued to rule – with the man she loved as little more than his cowed pet.

She could turn this aside, Aurora thought returning the globe to its box. She could go back to the hills and live as she always had. Free, as the Travelers were free. Content, with only her dreams to plague or stir her.

For life was precious. She rubbed the chill from her arms as she watched the last star wink out over Sorcerer's Mountain. Thane was right, life was precious. But she couldn't, wouldn't, turn away. For more precious than life was hope. And more precious than both was honor.

She woke Cyra and Rhiann to help her garb herself in the robes of a lady. She would wear the mask another day.

'Why don't you tell her?' Kern sat on a barrel eating a windfall apple while Thane fed the horses.

'There's nothing to tell.'

'Don't you think the lady would be interested in what you are, what you're doing. Or more what you don't?'

'She looks for heroes and warriors, as females do. She won't find one in me.'

'She . . . ' With a secret little smile, Kern munched his apple. 'Does not seem an ordinary female. Don't you wonder?'

Thane dumped oats in a trough. 'I can't afford to wonder. I put enough at risk last night because my blood was up. If she chatters about the tunnels, or what passed between us—'

'Does the lady strike you as a chatterbox?'

'No.' Thane rested his brow on a mare's neck. 'She is glorious. More than my dreams of her. Full of fire and beauty – and more, of truth. She won't speak of it, as she said she wouldn't. I wish I'd never seen her, touched her. Now that I have, every hour of the rest of my life is pain. If Owen chooses her . . . '

He set his teeth against a flood of black rage. 'How can I stay and watch them together? How can I go when I'm shackled here?'

'The time will come to break the shackles.'

'So you always say.' Thane straightened, moved to the next stall. 'But the years pass, one the same as the other.'

'The True One comes, Thane.'

'The True One.' With a mirthless laugh, he hauled up buckets of water. 'A myth, a shadow, to coat the blisters of Lorcan's rule with false hope. The only truth is the sword, and one day my hand will be free to use it.'

'A sword will break your shackles, Thane, but it isn't steel that will free the world. It is the midnight star.' Kern hopped off the barrel and laid a hand on Thane's arm. 'Take some joy before that day, or you'll never really be free.'

'I'll have joy enough when Lorcan's blood is on my sword.'

Kern shook his head. 'There's a storm coming, and you will ride it. But it will be your choice if you ride it alone.'

Kern flicked his wrist, and a glossy red apple appeared in his hand. With a merry grin, he tossed it to Thane, then vanished.

Thane bit into the apple, and the taste that flooded his mouth made him think of Aurora. He offered the rest to a greedy gelding.

Alone, he reminded himself, was best.

6

Wrapped in a purple cloak pinned with a jeweled brooch, Lorcan stood and watched his son practice his swordsmanship. What Owen lacked in style and form he made up for in sheer brutality, and that had his father's approval.

The soldier chosen for the practice had a good arm and a steady eye, and so made the match lively. Still, there were none in the city, or in the whole of Twylia, Lorcan knew, who could best the prince at steel against steel.

None would dare.

He had been given only one son, and that was a bitter disappointment. The wife he had taken in his youth had birthed two stillborn babes before Owen, and had died as she'd lived – without a murmur of complaint or wit – days after his birthing.

He had taken another, a young girl whose robust looks had belied a barren womb. It had been a simple matter to rid himself of her by damning her as a witch. After a month in the dungeons at the hands of his tribunal, she'd been willing enough to confess and face the purifying fires.

So he had taken Brynn. Far cousin of the one who had been queen. He'd wanted the blue of royal blood to run through the veins of his future sons – and had he got them, would have cast his firstborn aside without a qualm.

But Brynn had given him nothing but two daughters. Leia, at least, had possessed beauty, and would have been a rich bargaining chip in a marriage trade. But she'd been willful as well, and had tried to run away when he'd betrothed her.

The wild beasts of the forest had left little more than her torn and bloody cloak.

So he had no child but Dira, a pale, silent girl whose only use would be in the betrothing of her to a lord still loyal enough, still rich enough, to warrant the favor in two or three years' time.

He had planted his seed in Brynn again and again, but she lost the child each time before her term was up, and now was too sickly to breed. Even the maids and servants he took to his bed failed to give him a son.

So it was Owen who would carry his name, and his ambitions turned to the grandsons he would get. A king could not be a god without the continuity of blood.

His son must choose well.

He smiled as he watched Owen draw blood from his opponent, as he beat back his man with vicious strikes until the soldier lost his footing and fell. And Lorcan nodded with approval as Owen stabbed the sword's point into the man's shoulder.

He'd taught his son well. A fallen enemy was, after all, still an enemy.

'Enough.' Lorcan's rings flashed in the sunlight as he clapped his hands. 'Bear him away, bind him up.' He waved off the wounded soldier and threw his arm around Owen's shoulders. 'You please me.'

'He was hardly worth the effort.' Owen studied the stain on his blade before ramming it home. 'It's tedious not to have more of a challenge.'

'Come, the envoys have brought the taxes from the four points, and I would speak with you before I deal with them. There are rumbles of rebellion in the north.'

'The north is a place of ignorant peasants and hill dwellers who wait for Draco to fly from his mountain.' With a glance toward the high peak, Owen snorted in disgust. 'A battalion of troops sent up to burn a few huts, put a few of their witches on the pyre should be enough to quiet them.'

'The talk that comes down is not of Draco but of the True One.'

Owen's mouth twisted as he gripped the hilt of his sword. 'Tongues won't flap of what is forbidden once they are cut out. Those who speak of treason must be routed out and reminded there is only one king of Twylia.'

'And so they shall be. The envoys brought six rebels, as well as the taxes. They will be tried, and executed, as an example, as part of your betrothal ceremonies. Until then, the tribunal will . . . interrogate them. If these are more than rumbles, we will silence them.'

They strode through the gates of the castle and across the great hall. 'Meanwhile, preparations for the rest of the ceremonies proceed. You must make your choice within the week.'

Inside the throne room, Owen plucked a plum from a bowl and threw himself into a chair. 'So many plums.' He bit in, smiled. 'All so ripe and tasty.'

'There's more to your choice than a pleasing face. You may take any who stirs your blood into your bed. You are the prince, and will be king. Your bedmates may slake your lust, but your queen must do that and more. You must have sons.'

Lorcan poured wine, and sat by the fire that burned even so early in the day for his comfort. 'Strong sons, Owen. So you must choose a woman who will be more than a pretty vessel. Have any here found your favor?'

'One or two.' Owen shrugged. 'The latest arrival interests me. She has a bold look in her eye.'

'Her dowry would be rich,' Lorcan considered. 'And her father's lands are valuable. She has beauty enough, and youth. It might do.'

'The match would tie the west to us, and as Ute's land runs north along the hills, such positioning would be strategic.'

'Yes, yes.' Lorcan rested his chin on his fist and considered. 'The Realm of Magicks still thrives in pockets of the west, and too many men run tame there who preach of Draco's spell and the True One. It's time to look to the far west and north, and smother any small embers of treason before they flare.'

'The Lady Aurora's father, it seems, is unwell.' Owen took another bite of his plum. 'If we were wed, he might sicken and die – with a bit of help. And so his lands, his fortifications, his wealth would come to me.'

'It might do,' Lorcan repeated. 'I'll take a closer look at this one. If I approve, your betrothal will be announced at week's end at the masque. And you will be pledged the following morning.'

Owen raised a brow. 'So quickly?'

'With the wedding ceremony to take place at the end of a fortnight – by which time every man in the world must render a token to mark the events – the masque and the wedding. The shepherd must render his finest rams, the farmer one quarter of his crop, the miller a quarter of his grain, and so on, so as to provide their prince and his bride with the stores for their household.'

Lorcan stretched his booted feet toward the fire. 'If the man has no ram, no crop, no grain, he must render his oldest son or if he has no son, his oldest daughter, to serve the royal couple. Craftsmen and artisans will bequeath a year of their time so that your home can be built on the western border and furnished as befits your rank.'

'Some will not give willingly,' Owen pointed out.

'No. And the business of persuading them to do their duty to their king will bury all mutterings of the True One, scatter rebellious forces, and forge our hold on the west. Yes.' He lifted his goblet in toast. 'I think it may do.'

Under the guise of serving his mistress, Rohan walked with his head humbly bowed. His heart was full of rage edged in fear. He kept his eyes lowered as he moved past guards and into the sitting room where Aurora gathered with the women to take rose tea and chatter about gowns and the upcoming masque.

'Your pardon, my lady.'

Knowing her part, Aurora spared him a single disinterested glance. 'I am occupied.'

'I beg your pardon, my lady, but the lace you requested has arrived.'

'A full day late.' She set her cup aside and shook her head at the women who sat closest to her as she rose. 'It will probably be inferior, but we'll see what can be done with it. Have it sent to my chambers. I'll come now.'

She walked out behind him, careful not to speak to him or to Rhiann, who followed in her wake, until they were behind doors again.

'Lace.' She sighed heavily, and poured ale to rid her mouth of the oversweet taste of the rose tea. 'How I am lowered.'

'Lorcan's envoys returned today with taxes levied against the four points.'

Aurora's mouth thinned. 'He will not keep them for long.'

'They brought also six prisoners.'

'Prisoners? What prisoners are these?'

'They say they are rebels, but four are only farmers, and one of them is aged and near crippled, while another is no more than a boy. The other two must have been set upon and taken while scouting. One of them is Eton.'

Aurora lowered herself slowly to a chair as Rhiann bit back a cry. 'Our Eton? Cyra's betrothed?'

'Eton was wounded, and all are being kept in the dungeons.' He curled his hands helplessly into fists. 'They're to be questioned by the tribunal.'

'Tortured,' Aurora whispered.

'It's said they'll be executed for treason within the week. Flogged and branded, then hanged.'

'Compose yourself, Rhiann,' Aurora ordered when the woman began to weep. 'It will not happen. Why were they taken, Rohan? How are they charged with treason?'

'I can't say. There's word among the servants that rebellion is brewing, that the True One is coming.'

'So Lorcan strikes before he is struck.' She pushed to her feet to pace as she brought the positioning of the dungeons into her mind. 'We must get them out, and we will. We have a week.'

'You can't leave them there for a week.' Rhiann struggled against fresh tears. 'To be tortured and starved.'

'I have no choice but to leave them until we are ready to attack. If we try to free them now, we could fail, and even if we succeed, such a move would put Lorcan on alert.'

'Eton may be dead in a week,' Rhiann snapped. 'Or worse than dead. Is this how you honor your family?'

'This is how I rule, and it is bitter to me. Eton is like my own brother. Would you have me risk all to spare him?'

'No.' Rohan answered before Rhiann could speak. 'It would not honor him if you spared him pain, or even his life, and Lorcan continued to rule.'

'Get word to him if you can. Tell him he must hold on until we can find a way. Send a dispatch to Gwayne. It's time. They are to travel in secret. They must not be seen. How long will it take them? Three days?'

'Three – or four.'

'It will take three,' Aurora said firmly. 'I will meet him in the forest, near the tunnel, at midnight when he arrives. I'll know what must be done.'

'Cyra.' Rhiann grieved for her daughter. 'How will we keep this from her?'

'We won't. She has a right to know. I'll tell her. She should hear it from me.'

She went out in search of her friend, hoping she would have the right words, and met Owen as she stepped into the courtyard.

'Lady Aurora.' He took her hand, bowed over it. 'I was about to send word for you.'

'I am at your pleasure, my lord prince.'

'Then you'll honor me by riding out with me. I've been busy with matters of state all morning, and wish for a brisk gallop and your lovely company.'

'I would enjoy nothing more. May I meet you in an hour, my lord, so I might find my maid and change into proper attire?'

'I'll wait. Impatiently.'

She curtsied, tipping her face up with a saucy smile before rising and hurrying away. She found Cyra in the kitchens, her eyes bright and round with gossip.

'I require you,' Aurora said coolly, then turned away so that Cyra had to rush after her.

'I've learned all about—'

'Not now,' Aurora said under her breath. 'I'm riding out with the prince,' she said in a clear voice. 'I'll want my red riding habit, and be quick about it.'

'Yes, my lady.'

Only Aurora heard Cyra's muffled giggle as the girl rushed ahead to the bedchamber. And only Aurora hoped she would hear Cyra's laughter again.

'And be quick about it,' Cyra mimicked with another giggle as soon as Aurora closed the door behind her. 'I had to bite my lip to keep from laughing. Oh, Aurora, I've learned all manner of things. The kitchens are fertile ground.'

'Cyra, sit down. I must speak with you.'

The tone had Cyra stopping to look at Aurora as she lifted up the red habit. 'Do you not ride out with Owen, then?'

'No. Yes, that is – yes.' Aurora pushed at her hair. 'Yes, within the hour.'

'It'll take nearly that long to get this done. A lady of your station would have her hair dressed differently for riding. It has to suit the hat, you know. We'll get started and exchange our news. Oh, Aurora, mine is *so* romantic.'

'Cyra.' Aurora took the habit and tossed it aside so she could grasp Cyra's hand. 'I have word of Eton.'

'Eton? What of Eton? He's in the north, scouting for Gwayne.' The rosy flush was dying on her cheeks as she spoke, and her fingers trembled in Aurora's. 'Is he dead? Is he dead?'

'No. But he's hurt.'

'I'll go to him. I have to go to him.'

'You can't. Cyra.' She pushed her friend into a chair, then crouched at her feet. 'Eton and five others were taken by Lorcan's soldiers. He was wounded. I don't know how badly. He was brought here, to the dungeons.'

'He's here, in the castle? Now? And he lives?'

'Yes. They will question him. Do you know what that means?'

'They will torture him. Oh.' Cyra squeezed her eyes shut. 'Oh, my love.'

'I can do nothing for him yet. If I try . . . all could be lost, so I can do nothing yet. I'm sorry.'

'I need to see him.'

'It isn't safe.'

'I need to see him. They send food down to the jailers, to the tribunal, and slop to the prisoners. One of the kitchen maids will let me take her place. If he sees me, he'll know there's hope. It will make him stronger. He would never betray you, Aurora, and neither will I. He's proud to serve you, and so am I.'

Tears swam into Aurora's eyes, then she pressed her face into Cyra's lap. 'It hurts to think of him there.'

'Then you must not think of it.' She stroked Aurora's hair and knew that she herself would think of little else. 'I will pray for him. You'll be a good queen because you can cry for one man when so much depends on you.'

Aurora lifted her head. 'I'm so afraid. It comes close now, and I'm so afraid that I'll fail. That I'll die. That others will die for me.'

'If you weren't afraid, you'd be like Lorcan.'

Aurora wiped her eyes. 'How?'

'He isn't afraid because he doesn't love. To cause such pain you can't love or fear, but only crave.'

'Cyra, my sister.' Aurora lifted Cyra's hand and pressed it to her cheek. 'You've become wise.'

'I believe in you, and it makes me strong. You must change or you'll be late and annoy Owen. You need to keep him happy. It will make his death at your hands all the sweeter.'

Aurora's eyes widened. 'You talk easily of killing.'

'So will you, when I tell you what I've learned. Hurry. This will take some time.'

7

'Bryn was one of your mother's women, and her friend,' Cyra began.

'I know this. Now she sits as queen. Though not happily, by all appearances.' Aurora turned so Cyra could unhook her gown.

'She – Brynn – was widowed in the great battle. Thane was but three. In the year that followed, Lorcan decided to take a new wife. It's said – whispered – that she refused him but that he gave her the choice between giving herself to him and her son's life.'

'He would murder a child to win a wife?'

'He wanted Brynn, because she was closest to the queen, in spirit and in blood.' Cyra helped Aurora into the riding habit and began to fasten it. 'I only know it's said that Brynn wept to another of the handmaidens – the mother of the kitchen girl who spoke to me. She swore her allegiance, and gave herself to Lorcan for his promise to spare her son's life.'

Aurora sat at the dressing table, staring at her own face, and asked herself what she would have done. What any woman would have done. 'She had no choice.'

'Thane was sent to the stables, to work, and was not allowed inside the castle from that day, nor to speak a single word to his mother.'

'Hard, hard and cold. He could have taken Brynn by force and killed the boy. He kept him alive, kept Thane alive and within her reach, never to touch or speak. To make them both suffer, to cause pain for the sake of it. Payment,' Aurora said aloud as she let herself drift into the nightmare of Lorcan's mind. 'Payment for her first refusal of him.'

'This is his way,' Cyra agreed. 'A way of vengeance and retribution. Brynn married Lorcan, and twice miscarried his child before she gave birth to a daughter, who was Leia. Three years after, she bore Dira.'

'She had no choice, but Thane ... he's no longer a child.'

'Wait, there's more.' Cyra brushed out Aurora's hair and began to braid it. 'When Thane was but seven, he ran away – to join the rebels, it's said. He and a young friend. They were caught and brought back. The other boy, the brother of the maid who told me, was hanged.'

The horror of it cut through her heart. 'By Draco, he hanged a half-grown boy?'

'And forced Thane to watch it done. Thane was beaten and told that if he insulted the king again, another would die in his place. And still he ran away, less than a year later. He was captured, brought back, beaten, and another boy his age was hanged.'

'This is beyond evil.' Aurora bowed her head. 'Beyond madness.'

'And more yet. Lorcan took the baby, Dira, his own daughter and half sister to Thane, to the stables where Thane was shackled. She was only days old. And he put his own dagger at the baby's throat. If Thane ran again, if he spoke ill of Lorcan or Owen, if he disobeyed any law or displeased the king in any way, Dira would die for it, then Leia, then Brynn herself. If he did not submit, any and all who shared his blood would be put to death.'

'Could he kill his own?' Struggling to see it, Aurora rubbed a hand over her troubled heart. 'Yes, yes, he could do

247

it. She is only a female child, after all,' she said bitterly. 'And how could a brother, a boy, a man, risk it? He could run, and now he could escape, but he could never forfeit his sisters' lives, risk his mother's.'

She thought of what she'd seen in the crystal. The wolf walking like a tame dog, while his mother and sister were chained to the throne. And the ghost of another sister stood trapped behind glass. 'No, he could not run, he could not fight. Not even for his own freedom.'

'He never did so again,' Cyra confirmed as she rolled the braid into a thick knot at the base of Aurora's neck. 'He speaks little to others, stays among the horses.'

'He makes no friends,' Aurora said quietly, 'except a girl in a vision and an aged faerie. Because to make friends puts them at risk. So he's always alone.'

'It breaks my heart.' Cyra dashed a tear from her cheek. 'They think he's beaten – Lorcan, Owen, everyone. But I don't believe this is so.'

'No.' She remembered how he'd looked in the forest with a sword in his hand and the cold fire of battle in his eyes. 'It is not so. He has buried his pride and given more than half his life to the waiting, but he is not beaten.' She reached back to take Cyra's hand. 'Thank you for telling me.'

'A man who would humble himself to save another is a great man, greater perhaps than one who fights.'

'Stronger. Truer. I misjudged him because I didn't look beyond my own eyes, into my heart. This wolf is not tamed. He stalks. I have fresh hope.' She got to her feet, turned. 'Go see your man, but take care. Take great care. Tell him, if you can, it won't be long. Three days, no more than four, and we will bring a flood to the City of Stars. I swear on my life, Lorcan will drown in it.'

She stepped in front of the looking glass, and her smile was a warrior's smile. 'Now we'll go flutter and preen for the son of the devil, and see what use he is to us.'

Aurora hurried to the stables, hoping for a moment alone with Thane. Her horse and Owen's were already saddled. Owen's personal guard stood at the riding gelding's head.

She moved to her own mount as if inspecting the horse and the tack.

'You, there.' She approached the stables, clapped her hands imperiously. 'Stableboy!'

Thane stepped out. He kept his head lowered, but his eyes lifted, and the hot resentment in them blasted her face. 'My lady.'

For the benefit of the guard, she crooked a finger and moved to her mount's far hind leg. She bent as if to inspect the knee, and as Thane did the same, she whispered. 'I must speak with you. Tonight. I'll come to the stables.'

'There is nothing more to say, and you put yourself and me at risk.'

'It's urgent.' Risking a touch, she brushed her fingers over the back of his hand. 'Beloved.'

She heard the clatter of armor and sword as the guard snapped to attention. Giving her horse a light pat, she straightened and turned to smile at Owen.

'Do you have some trouble with this ... thing?' Owen demanded, sneering at Thane.

'Indeed, no, my lord. My mount seemed to favor this leg when we rode in. I was complimenting your boy on the care of my horse. I'm very fond of my horse.' Deliberately, she reached into her purse and drew out a copper. 'For your good work,' she said and handed the coin to Thane.

'Thank you, my lady.'

'It isn't necessary to give him coin, nor to speak to him.'

'I find such small boons ensure good care.' She moved, subtly, so that she stood between Thane and Owen, and sent the prince her brightest smile. 'As I said, I'm very fond of my horse. Will you help me mount, my lord? I am so looking forward to a gallop.'

Owen shoved the mounting block aside and set his hands

on Aurora's waist. She laid hers on his shoulders and let out a flirtatious laugh as he vaulted her into the saddle.

'You're very strong, my lord.' She gathered her reins. 'I also have a fondness for a strong man.' With another laugh, she clicked her tongue and sent her horse flying away from the stables.

Owen, she discovered, was a mediocre rider on a superior mount. She reined herself in to keep pace with him. It was good, despite the choice of company, to ride. To feel the freshness of the air on her skin and to be away from the clatter of the castle and the smells of the city.

Her men, she thought, would come from the northwest, using the forest for cover and keeping off the roads. Then the hills would ring with the battle and, when it was done, with victory.

'You look thoughtful, Aurora.' Owen studied her as they slowed to a trot at the edge of field and forest.

'Only admiring the beauty of this country, my lord. And wondering how pleasant it is to know that all you see is yours.'

'The woman I choose will have part in that.'

'If you will it,' she said carelessly, and walked her horse along the forest path. 'There is rich land in the west, as well. My father tends what's his with a firm hand and a clear eye. The hills reach high there, and the cattle grow fat on them.'

'The name of my bride will be announced at the masque, at week's end.'

'So I am told.' She slid her gaze toward his, quirked her lips. And slid her power over him like silk. 'Do you know it?'

'Perhaps I do.' He reached to take her reins and stop her horse, then leapt from his own. While she raised her eyebrows, he circled, then lifted his arms to pluck her from the saddle. 'But a prince must take care in selecting a bride. One who will be queen.'

She laid her hand on his chest. 'So he must – as a woman must take care, my lord, in who takes her favors.'

'I want a woman who will stir my blood.' He pulled her closer and would have taken her mouth if she hadn't laid her fingers on his lips.

'A man's blood is easily stirred. And if a woman gives him what he desires before a pledge is made, the woman is a fool. What man, what king, wants a foolish wife?'

'If you give me what I desire, and it pleases me, I will make the pledge. Lie with me now, and you will be queen.'

'Make me queen.' She played her fingers along his jaw. 'And I will lie with you. I will give you sons, and great pleasure in the making of them.'

'I could take you.' He dug his fingers into her hips. 'You couldn't stop me.' His breath came short as he lifted her to her toes. 'You belong to me, as every blade of grass in the field beyond belongs to me. I am your lord. I am your god.'

'You have the strength, and the power.' And though she had a dagger beneath her skirts, she couldn't afford to use it, not even in defense against rape. 'Why take by force today what would be given freely in a few days' time?'

'For excitement.'

She only laughed, and tapped his cheek. 'To hump like rabbits in the dirt? Hardly befitting you, my lord, or the woman who wishes to sit by your side, and lie by it. The waiting will, I think . . .' She traced her fingertip over his lips. 'Hone appetites.'

'A sample, then.' He circled her throat with his hand, squeezed, then covered her lips with his in a brutal kiss. She tasted his desire, and his delight in force. With all her will she swallowed revulsion and fury, and let him take.

She thought of how he would pay for this, and for the thousands of cruelties to her people, for his part in humiliating Thane. For every lash Eton might suffer.

When his hands pawed at her, when they clamped bruisingly on her breasts, she neither struggled nor winced. For he would pay.

'My lord, I beg you.' She hoped the quaver in her voice could be taken for passion rather than the rage she felt. 'Indulge me and wait for the rest. You will not be disappointed, I promise.'

'Would you rather I nibble some housemaid to sate my appetite?'

'Such a man as you would have great appetites. I will do my best to meet them, at the proper time.' She broke free. 'Your kisses make me tremble. It will break my heart if you only toy with me.'

He grasped her waist and tossed her up to the saddle more roughly than necessary. 'You'll know my answer at week's end.'

Bastard, she thought as she gathered her reins. But she smiled, with her lashes lowered. 'And you, my lord, will know mine.'

She wanted to bathe, to rub her lips raw so that there was nothing left of the taste or feel of him. But she laughed and talked her way through another night of feasting. She lifted her cup to the king in toast. She danced, and pretended only feminine flusters and objections when Owen pulled her into the shadows and touched her body. As if he had the right.

Her mind was too troubled to speak of it to Rhiann as

she removed the ball gown and put on her nightdress. She watched the sky, careful not to venture too close to the window, as the world quieted toward sleep.

Then, donning cloak and hood, she slid out into the night, to the stables.

She knew he wasn't there. She understood now that part of her would sense him, would always sense him. So he hadn't waited for her, as she'd asked.

Once again she took a candle and followed after him through the tunnels, and into the forest beyond.

He stood in the moonlight. It showered over his ragged shirt, his unkempt hair, the worn boots.

'I told you not to come.'

'I need to speak with you.' She blew the candle out, set it down. 'To see you. To be with you.'

He stepped back. 'Are you mad, or simply sent here to ensure I will be?'

'You could have told me when I asked why you stay here.'

'It's nothing to do with you.'

'Everything you do, everything you are, and think and feel, all of you has to do with all of me.'

'You rode with him.'

'I do what needs to be done, as you do. Thane.' She reached out a hand as she moved to him, but he turned away.

'Will you be wedded to him, and bedded to him? Does that need to be done?'

For the first time in days a smile that came from her heart curved her lips. 'You're jealous. I'm small enough to enjoy that. He will never have me as a man has a woman. You already have.'

'I haven't. I won't.'

'In dreams you have.' She moved in, laid her cheek on his back and felt his body go taut as a bowstring. 'You've dreamed of me.'

Both heart and body strained toward her. 'All of my life, it seems, I've dreamed of you.'

'You love me.'

'All of my life.' He spun back, held her at arm's length when she would have embraced him. 'You kept me alive, I think, in dreaming of you. The loving of you, and being loved. Now, by the gods, you'll be the death of me.'

'No one lives forever.' She took off her cloak, spread it on the ground. Then, standing in the moonlight, she drew off her nightdress, let it pool at her feet. 'Live now.'

He reached out, wound her long, dark hair around his

fist. He could walk away from this, still had the strength. Or he could take love, one precious moment of love, and have its comfort and torment with him the rest of his days.

'If hell awaits me, I'll have one night in heaven first.'

'We'll have it.' She waved a hand and around them cast a circle of protective fire. The light of it shimmered in golds as a thin mist covered the ground in a pure white blanket.

'I've waited for you, Thane.' She touched her lips to his, fit her body to his. 'Through the light, and through the dark.'

'For this one night with you, I would trade a thousand nights alone. Bear a thousand lashes, die a thousand deaths.'

'Midnight nears.' She smiled as he lowered her to the soft and misted ground. 'It's my hour.'

'It will be ours. Aurora.' He kissed her tenderly, very tenderly. 'My light.'

Sweet, so sweet, that merging of lips, the brush of fingertips over flesh. She knew his taste, his touch, so warmly familiar, and yet so gloriously new. The feel of his body, the hard muscle, the ridged scars, aroused her, as did the gleam of his eyes in the glow of witch fire.

'Thane. My wolf.' With a laugh, she reared up and nipped at his chin. 'So much better than a dream.'

Their lips met again, a deep search that had her trembling

beneath him, and shifting restlessly as needs heated in her blood. Her heart thundered under his palm – the hard callus of his labors, then under his mouth – the hot brand of his need. And her belly began to ache as if with hunger. Her own hands became more demanding, tugging at his worn shirt. The sound of cloth ripping was only another thrill.

He wanted to go slowly, to draw this night into forever. She could vanish, he knew, when the sun struck, and he would be left with more misery than he thought he could bear.

But his need for her was impossible, enormous, and the love that stormed through him stole his breath. The urgency built with every touch, every murmur, until he was half mad.

Whatever he took, she gave, then only demanded more. She cried out his name when he drove her to peak, then clung relentlessly with her mouth like a fever on his.

The empty well of his life flooded full, and he knew for the first time something he would kill to keep.

His hands clamped on her wrists. He looked down at her with eyes fierce and gleaming green. 'You'll never belong to him. He'll never touch you like this.'

'No.' Here was power, she realized. Another kind of female power. 'Only you. It is the woman who gives herself to you, and only you.' She heard the bells begin to strike the hour. 'Mate with me, join with me. Love with me. We'll be more together than either can be alone.'

He plunged inside her, watched the power and the pleasure of the moment rush over her face. And felt the rough magic of it whip through him.

Then she was moving under him and with him, and for him. Their fingers locked, their lips met.

Overhead, lightning flashed in the form of a dragon, and the stars flared red as blood.

8

When the witching hour passed, she stayed with him. But she knew the time grew short. If they were as others, she mused, they could remain like this, wrapped warm in her cloak, and sleep until dawn broke.

But they were not as others.

'I have much to tell you,' she began.

He only drew her closer to his side. 'You're a witch. I know. I'm bewitched. And grateful.'

'I've cast no spell on you, Thane.'

He smiled and continued to study the stars. 'You are the spell.'

'We are the spell.' She shifted so she could look down at his face. 'I'll explain. You are a hero to me.'

He looked away from her and started to move.

'A man who would put all he wanted, all he needed, aside to protect others? The greatest of warriors. But that time is ending.' She took his hand, brought it to her lips. 'Will you stand beside me? Will you pledge me your sword?'

'Aurora, I will pledge you my life. But I won't lift a sword knowing the act will bring another down on my sister. My mother. Or some poor innocent. They hanged my friend, and he was but six seasons. His only crime was in following me.'

'I know.' She kissed his cheek. 'I know.' And the other. 'No harm will come to your family, or to any in your stead.' She reached out, picked up her dagger, and drew it across her palm. 'I swear it, on my blood.'

He gripped her hand. 'Aurora—'

'She is my sister now. She is my mother now. You are my husband now.'

Emotion stormed across his face. 'You would take me this way? I'm nothing.'

'You're the bravest man I know, and you're mine. You are the most honorable, and the most true. Will you take me?'

The world, Thane thought, could change in one magic hour. 'I'll get you away to safety. I know how it can be done, with Kern's help—'

'I go nowhere.'

'To the Valley of Secrets, through the Realm of Magicks,' he continued, ignoring her protest. 'My sister is safe there, and so will you be.'

'Your sister? Leia lives?'

Fury flashed onto his face. 'He would have sold her, like a mare. Bartered her like a whore. She was but sixteen. With Kern's help, she was taken from the castle and away, and her cloak left torn and bloodied deep in the woods. She lives, and I will owe Kern and his kind all of my days. But she is lost to me, and I can't risk getting word of her to my mother, to give her even that much comfort.'

Not a ghost, Aurora realized, but a memory. Shielded and safe – and apart. She touched her fingers to his cheeks. 'What did it cost you?' she murmured.

'Kern asked for no payment.'

'No – what did Lorcan and Owen take from you? What scars do you bear from their anger at the loss of so valuable a possession to them? So many times, when we came to each other in visions, I saw your sadness. But you would never tell me.'

'You would always bring me joy. Beloved.'

'They whipped you in her stead. Laid the lash on your back because they couldn't lay it on hers. I can see it now, and that you reached through the pain, beyond it, because your sister was saved.'

'Don't look.' He gripped her hands when her smoky eyes went dark with vision. 'There's no pain here now. And there will be none. Kern will help me get you away. You, and my mother and sister, your women. Then I'll find the rebels, and come back to deal with Lorcan and his whelp.'

'You won't have to look far for the rebels. They're on their way even now. Your mother and your sister will be safe. I've sworn it. But I stay, and I fight.' She laid her hands on his shoulders to stem his protest, and looked deep into his eyes. 'A queen does not sit in safety while others win the world.'

She got to her feet. 'I am Aurora, daughter of Gwynn and Rhys. I am the Lady of the Light. I am the True One, and my time has come. Will you stand with me, Thane the Valiant, and pledge me your sword?'

There was a light around her as she spoke, as gold as sunlight and stronger than the witch fire she'd conjured. For a moment it seemed a crown of stars sat sparkling on her head, and their brilliance was blinding.

He had to struggle to find his voice, but he knelt. 'My lady. I never believed in you, and still I knew you from my first breath. All that I have, all that I am is yours. I would die for you.'

'No.' She dropped to her knees to take his face in her hands. 'You must live for me. And for the child we made tonight.' She took his hand and pressed it to her belly.

'You can't know—'

'I do. I do know.' Her face, her voice, were radiant. 'You gave me a child tonight, and he will be king, and rule this world after us. He will be more than either of us, more still than the sum of us. We must win it back for him, and for our people. We will take from Lorcan, in blood if we must, what he took in blood. But you must live for me, Thane. Swear it.'

'I swear it.' In all of his memory he'd lived with nothing. Now in one night he was given the world. 'A son?'

'For the first. We will make others.' With a laugh, she threw her arms around him. 'They will be happy, and so well loved. And they will serve, Thane.' She drew back. 'Serve the world as well as rule it. This can be. I begin to see so much of what can be. I needed you to clear my vision.'

'How many come? What are their arms?'

'Now you think like a soldier.' Satisfied, she sat on the

ground. 'I'll know more soon. Here, at midnight the night after next, we meet Gwayne. He is my hawk, and he brings the forces. Two of mine are held now in the dungeon. One is as dear as a brother to me. They must be freed, but not until the night of the masque. I pray they live to see that night, and they are not to be sacrificed.'

'I can get them out. I know the tunnels and underground better than any. There are others held there who would stand with you.'

'What do you need?'

'One good man and his sword would be enough.'

'You shall have him. This must be done, and quietly, in the hour before the masque. The wounded, or those too weak to fight, must be taken through the tunnels and away. Men will die, Thane. There will be no choice. But I want no man's blood spilled carelessly. Some would swear allegiance if given the opportunity. From what I've seen, not all who serve Lorcan do so with a full heart.'

'Some serve only in fear of their lives or the lives of their loved ones.' He shrugged when she studied him. 'Men often speak their mind around horses. And minions.'

'You are no one's minion.'

'I've been less than that.' His hand curled into a fist. 'By the blood, for the first time since childhood I know what it is to want, more than to live, to stretch out of this skin and be. I would have served you,' he said quietly. 'I have seen you wear the Crown of Stars, and I would have served you in anything you asked, servant to queen. But to have loved you, as a man loves a woman, has changed everything. I can never go back.'

'Only for a short time. My wolf will conceal his fangs only for a short time. I must go now. When we move, Thane, we must move quickly.' She went willingly into his arms, held close. 'We'll have all of our lives for the rest.'

And for the rest, he thought, as he let her go, she and the child would be protected at any and all costs.

Hoping to avoid Owen for the day, Aurora made plans to go into the city and there measure the feeling among the people – and the strategy of attack and defense. It was difficult to deny herself a trip to the stables and even a fleeting moment with Thane, but she sent Rohan to order the carriage, as was fitting for a lady of her station.

'Soon there will be no more need for pretense. Or the wait,' she added and touched Cyra's shoulder. 'The prisoners will be freed, and the wounded among them taken safely into the forest. I promise you.'

'He suffers, Aurora. My Eton suffers. I could barely stand

to see him so. Many held there don't even know their crime, and some are driven mad by the dark and the starvation.'

'It won't be dark much longer. Men held there have fathers or sons or brothers. They'll fight with me. I saw the dragon in the sky last night, and the red stars.' She laid a hand on her belly. 'I've seen what can be.'

She hooked her arm with Cyra's and started across the courtyard. And heard the clash of armor as guards snapped to attention.

The heat of battle flashed in her blood even as she bowed her head and curtsied to the man who called himself king.

'Majesty.'

He took her hand to bring her to her feet, and didn't release it. 'A pretty light on a gloomy morning.'

'You are too kind, sire. But even a dank day in such a place is a joy.'

'And do you ride out again today?'

'I go into the city, with your permission, my lord, in hopes to find something appropriate for the masque. I don't wish to dishonor you or the prince by arriving at such a spectacle in my country garb.'

'You go unescorted, lady?'

'I have my men, sir, and my women.' She fluttered up at him. 'Will I not be safe enough?'

He chucked her under the chin and made her spine freeze. 'Beauty is never safe enough. Do you not seek the company of the prince?'

'Always, my lord. But . . .' She offered a slow, sidelong smile. 'I fear he may become bored with me if I am too accessible. Do you not think that a man desires a woman more when she is just out of reach?'

'You're a clever one, aren't you?'

'A clever mind is a valuable tool to a woman. As is amiability, so if you prefer I forgo this venture and wait upon Prince Owen's pleasure, I will do so.' She glanced over as Rohan brought her carriage into the courtyard. 'Shall I send it away again, sire?'

'Go, and enjoy. I look forward to seeing what catches your eye in the shops.' He helped her into the carriage, and was obviously pleased when she peeked out the window and sent him one last smile.

'He makes my skin crawl,' Aurora said as she flopped back against the seat.

'He would have you for himself if he could.' Rhiann nodded wisely. 'There's a look in a man's eye when he imagines such things. Having you for his son is his next choice.'

'What he'll have is my sword at his throat. And a happy

day that will be. How much have we left to spend?' she demanded.

Rhiann carefully counted out the coins in her purse, and had Aurora blowing out a breath.

'I hate to waste it on foolishness, but I have to make a showing. Lorcan will expect it now.'

'You can be very particular,' Cyra said, and worked up a smile. 'Turning up your nose at the offerings, sniffing at materials, waving away baubles.'

'I suppose. I'd rather be inside the taverns listening to the talk, but we'll leave that to Rohan.' She glanced out the window of the carriage, and her heart ached at the sight of children begging for food. She thought of the taxes levied, all the coins stored inside the palace.

'I have an idea, something that might distract Lorcan and help our army move into the forest unnoticed. Chaos,' she declared, 'is another kind of weapon.'

Furious, Owen stalked into the stables. He'd wanted Aurora, but she was off – with no word to him – to the city. He'd planned another ride, with a picnic by the river. And a seduction.

If he were to choose her, and his mind was nearly made up, he expected her to be available at his whim. It was best she learned that now.

There were others with more beauty, others with more generous attributes. If she refused to come to heel, he would take one of them as queen, and make the intriguing Aurora a consort.

He pushed his way into a stall where Thane was wrapping a foreleg for the mount of one of the soldiers.

'Saddle my horse.'

Thane kept his head lowered as he continued to wrap the leg. 'Yes, my lord.'

'Now, you worthless nit.' He struck out, slapping Thane in the face with the back of his hand.

Thane took the blow, and though he knew it was foolish, he checked his grip on the halter so that the frightened horse shied and canted, driving Owen into the wall of the stall.

'You'll pay for that, you ham-handed bastard.'

There was enough satisfaction in watching Owen go white as bone and scramble out of the stall to take all the sting out of the next blow. 'A thousand pardons, my lord prince.'

'I'll deal with you later. Get my horse, and be quick about it.'

As Owen strode out of the stables, Thane grinned and wiped the blood from his mouth.

'The mount's wasted on him.' Thane turned and saw Kern leading the already saddled horse from its stall. 'A lame one-eyed donkey would be wasted on him.'

Thane ran a hand over the gleaming neck of Owen's stallion. 'If the gods are with me, and I live, I will have this horse as my own. Thank you for saddling him.'

'A simple matter, in a complicated time.'

'You knew who she was. Who she is.'

'The True One shines.'

'She does.' Thane rested his brow on the stallion's neck. 'I have such love for her. Fierce and frightening love. I'll do what needs to be done, Kern, but I ask you, whatever you've given me over the years, to give it now to my family. I can go into any battle, take any risk, if I know they're protected.'

'You've stood as their shield long enough. I'll stand for you when the time comes.'

'Then I'll be ready.' He led the horse out, and stood meekly at its head while Owen berated him.

'I'll be ready,' he repeated and watched Owen spur the mount and ride off.

The sky stayed dim, but no rain fell. Aurora watched the dark clouds and prayed that the storm brewing would hold while her men marched toward the city. She used her time there to study the fortifications, to watch the changing of the guard under the guise of wandering among the shops.

The wares were rich, and the people starving.

'There is talk,' Rohan told her as she stood by as if to supervise the loading of her goods into the carriage, 'of portents. The dragon flew in the sky last night, and the stars bled.'

'And what do the people make of these portents?'

'Some fear it's the end of the world, some hope it's the beginning.'

'They're both right.'

'But those who dare speak of hope do so in whispers. More were dragged from their homes in the night and charged with treason. There are murmurs, Aurora, that Lorcan will use the masque for some dark purpose, that he plans some sorcery.'

'He has no such powers.'

'It's said he has sought them.' Rohan glanced left, right, to be certain they weren't overheard. 'That he has courted the dark. Sacrifices. Human sacrifices to draw power from blood.'

'Superstitious mutterings. But we won't ignore them.' She climbed into the carriage and rode back to the castle with her mind circling a hundred thoughts.

There was a time for warriors, and a time for witches. When the hour was late, Aurora stirred her power. She called the hawk, and ten of his fellows. Then twenty, then a hundred. And more, until the sky teemed with them. Standing in her window, she raised the wind and, lifting her arms, threw her power into it.

Hawks screamed, circled, dove. Guards and courtiers rushed to the courtyard and the gardens, to the city, to the walls. There were cries of fear, shouts of wonder.

The great birds flew into the castle, through window and door, and sent servants scurrying under chair and bed. The beat of wings, the call of hawk, filled the air as in a golden mass they streaked into the treasury, plucking coins in their talons, streaming out again to drop them like rich rain on the city.

With cries of wonder and delight, men, women, and children rushed out of their homes and hovels to gather the bounty. When the call to arms came, many of the soldiers were as busy as the townspeople stuffing coins into pocket and purse. Before order could be restored, the cry of hawks was an echo, the beat of wings a memory.

The streets of the city glittered with coins.

An early payment, Aurora thought, watching the chaos below her window. The rest would come, very soon.

There was talk of little else the next day. Some blamed the strange raid on faeries, or witchcraft. It was said that the king's rage was black. Soldiers posted proclamations warning that any citizen found with coins would forfeit a hand.

Still, there was not a single coin left on the streets, and for the first time Aurora heard more laughter than woe when she listened to the city.

The confusion had kept her out of Lorcan's and Owen's way through the day, and given her time to have young Rhys slither into the dungeons with food for the prisoners while the guards gossiped.

But the time for giving food and coin to those in need was over, and the time for war was nearly upon her.

Distracted, she hurried toward her chamber to make final preparations for meeting Gwayne, and she didn't see Owen lurking. He had her back to the wall and his hand at her throat. She was already reaching for her dagger before caution had her fisting her hand and struggling to turn the battle light in her eye to fear.

'My lord. You frighten me.'

'What game do you play?'

She shivered and turned her lips up in a tremulous smile. 'Many, sir, and well. What have I done to displease you?'

'I did not give you leave to fritter off. Two days have

passed, and you have not sought my company. I did not give you leave to travel into the city yesterday.'

'No, my lord, but your father, the king, did so. I only sought the shops in hope that I might find something to please you for the ball. We have nothing so fine in the west as in the City of Stars. Please, my lord.' She touched her hand to his. 'You're hurting me.'

'I've made it clear that I favor you. If you don't wish me to turn my eye toward another, take care, Aurora.'

'Your favor, my lord, is all I could wish, but your passions unnerve me. I'm only a maid.'

'I can make you more.' He pushed his hand between her legs. 'And less.'

'Would you treat me so?' She wished for tears, willed them into her eyes as rage spewed through her. 'Like a doxy to be fondled in doorways? Do you show your favor by dishonoring me?'

'I take what I wish. When I wish.'

'My lady!' Rhiann screamed in shock and rushed down the corridor with Cyra at her heels.

Aurora broke away, to fall sobbing into Rhiann's arms and let herself be carried away into her chamber.

The minute the door was shut and secured, she stood dry-eyed. 'Speak of this to no one,' she ordered. 'No one.'

She looked at the hand she held close to her side, and the dagger in it. 'The prince of pigs has no idea how close he came to being gutted. I will not dine tonight. Send word that Lady Aurora is indisposed.'

She sat and picked up a quill. 'I have work.'

9

She wore a high-necked gown to hide the bruises in a color chosen to blend with the night. There was enough anger left from her encounter with Owen to have her strapping a short sword at her side as well as the dagger on her thigh.

She threw on her cloak, with her mother's brooch pinned inside it.

She carried no lamp or candle, but slipped like a shadow through the castle. At the sound of approaching footsteps, she pressed herself against the wall, and through the veil of witch smoke watched two guards lead a serving girl toward Owen's chambers. The girl's face was pale as the moon, and her eyes dull with fear and resignation.

Aurora's hand clamped on the hilt of her sword, her knuckles white with rage and impotence against the metal. She could not interfere, could do nothing to help the poor girl, for to do so would risk all.

But he would pay. She vowed it. As his father would pay for his treatment of innocence.

She hurried down the steps, easing through doorways, and slipped out of the castle through the kitchen. Drawing up her hood, she made her way to the stables under the cover of darkness.

The instant she was inside, Thane pulled her into his arms. 'I worry,' he whispered even as his lips sought hers. 'Every moment I can't see you, touch you, know you're safe, I worry.'

'It's the same for me.' She eased back, just to touch his face, and saw the bruises. 'Oh, Thane.'

'It's nothing. Nothing he won't pay for.'

Instinctively she touched the neck of her gown, thought of the marks of Owen's hand hidden under it. 'Payment will be made. I swear it. Come, and let's pray that Gwayne and our army await.'

He lifted the door to the tunnels, but when he reached for a lamp, Aurora stilled his hand. 'No. Tonight, we go by my light. It must be shown,' she said as she drew the crystal star from the pocket of her cloak. 'To give those who would fight hope, to let them see what they risk their lives for.'

The star shimmered, and the light within it grew until it pulsed pure white. It beamed through the dark of the tunnels and became as bright as day.

And she was the light, burning with the power and purity of it. His throat stung, and his heart swelled with a mixture of love and wonder. 'My lady. If my heart and my sword, if my life were not already yours, I would lay them before you now.'

'Keep your life, beloved, for a thousand stars would never light mine without you. I need my wolf.' She took his hand as they moved through the tunnels. 'My lord of the stables. You know more of courtly matters than I.'

At his quick laugh she shook her head. 'You do,' she insisted. 'I was raised as a Traveler – educated, it's true, by book, by battle, by journeys and song and story, but there will come a time when I must hold court. It plays on my nerves.'

'You are every inch a queen. It's a wonder men don't fall to their knees when you pass.'

'You love me.' And it warmed her to say it. 'So it would seem so to you. It won't just be a matter of defeating Lorcan, but of convincing the people of the world that I am true. The work is just beginning.'

'I'm used to work.'

It was Kern who waited at the end of the tunnel. He wore light armor and his battle sword. 'They come, Lady of the Light. But first, I bring you greetings from the Realm of Magicks.' He bowed low. 'And request to speak as envoy.'

'You are welcome, sir.' She glanced at Thane in confusion when Kern remained bowed.

Thane grinned, sent her a wink. He hadn't been tutored by a faerie throughout his life without learning the protocol. 'You do honor to your queen, Lord of Magicks. Greetings to you from the world of men. You have leave to speak.'

'Well done.' Kern rose with a twinkle in his eye.

'Meaning no offense, but can we speak freely here?' Aurora gestured with her free hand. 'Men and faerie folk share the forest, and the night. I am not queen until I'm crowned, and I have much yet to learn on how to be one. What word do you bring from your realm?'

'I have a lengthy and lyrical speech prepared.'

'Lengthy it would be,' Thane assured Aurora. 'I can't promise the lyrical.'

'However' – Kern shot his student a steely stare – 'I'll cut it to the bone. The Realm of Magicks is at your command, Lady of the Light. We will fight with you if you'll have us.'

'You haven't raised your forces or your powers against Lorcan in all these years. Why do you offer to raise them now?'

'We've raised your wolf, my lady, as it was written. I am for him, and he is for you. The hour to do more had not come.'

'Faeries can die at the hand of men – and more, it's said that Lorcan courts magic. Will you and yours risk all that is to come?'

'We have died at the hands of men, hands that follow Lorcan's command. And some of us have turned from truth to embrace the lies. Some from weakness, some from fear, and some from the ambition for greater powers. Our kinds are not so different in such matters, my lady. We will follow the queen into battle. Will the queen trust my word?'

Aurora turned to Thane. 'I'll trust yours.'

'He's as true as any I know.'

'Then thanks to you and your kind, Lord of Magicks. What you've said here tonight, and what you'll do on the morrow, will never be forgotten.'

He took the hand she offered, bowed over it. 'Your hawks provided fine entertainment in the night, Majesty.'

'There is little entertainment in this place. I craved some. And it served to keep Lorcan and his dogs' eyes on the city, and away from the forest.'

'Now your white hawk approaches.'

She swung around and saw Gwayne step away from the trees, alone. Regal protocol was forgotten in the sheer joy of seeing him. She sprang toward him, threw her arms around him. 'I've missed you! There's so much to say, and little time to say it.' She drew back, studied his face. 'You're tired.'

'It was a long journey.'

'How many are with you?'

'We're two hundred strong, but many of those are farmers, craftsmen. Boys.' He gripped her hands, squeezed. 'Some are armed with clubs, pitchforks, or simply stones from the fields, but they come.'

'Then they're valued for it, every one.'

'They need to see, Aurora, to believe, for they're weary, and some grow frightened. Without a stir of hope, some will scatter by morning.'

'They will see, and they will believe.' She reached back for Thane's hand. 'This is Thane, who is my mate, the wolf of my visions. And Kern of the faeries, who is his teacher and brings us word from his realm of their loyalty to the True One. Take us to the army, Gwayne, so they can see. And pray to the gods I find the words to stir them.'

Gwayne led them through the forest, calling a low signal to sentries already posted. The camp was rough, the faces of the men she saw pale with fatigue. Some were old, others much too young, and her heart began to ache with the knowledge of what she would ask of them.

She shook her head before Gwayne could speak. 'I must do this myself. If I can't do this, I can't do the rest. They have followed you this far, my hawk. Now they have to follow me.'

Gathering herself, she climbed onto a wide stump and stood quietly for a moment while the men shifted and murmured and studied her.

'I am Aurora.' She didn't lift her voice, but kept it low so the murmuring stilled as the men strained to hear. 'I am the Lady of the Light. I am the queen of Twylia. I am the True One. The woman I am weeps at what has been done to the world, to the people and the magicks of it. My father, the king, was slain through treachery, and my mother, the queen, gave her life for my birth. I am from death, and my heart bleeds knowing that more death will come from me. I am a woman, and have no shame of tears.'

She let them fall silently down her face and glimmer in the moonlight filtering through the trees.

'I am Aurora.' Her tone strengthened as she loosed her cape and flung it aside. As she drew her sword and raised it to the sky. 'I am the Lady of the Light. I am the queen of Twylia. I am the True One. The warrior in me burns at what has been done to the world, to the people and the magicks of it. I will not rest, I will fight unto death to take back what was stolen from me and mine. My sword will sing into battle. I am a warrior, and I have no fear of death when the cause is justice.'

Once more she held the crystal star in her palm and drew from it, from herself, the power of light. Men fell back, or dropped to their knees as that light grew and grew until it burned like a thousand candles. Wind whipped through the forest, sent her hair flying as she held both sword and star aloft.

'I am Aurora!' Her voice rang through the night, and the bells began their toll of midnight. 'I am the Lady of the Light. I am the queen of Twylia. I am the True One. I am a witch, and my rage for what has been done to the world and my people is cold as ice, is hot as flame, is deep as the sea. My power will light the dark, and it will blind those who stand against me. I am woman and warrior, witch and queen. I will weep and fight and blaze until the world is right again. And all who follow me will be remembered and honored until the end of days.'

She threw back her head and punched her power toward the sky. Light carved through the black, and spun in mad circles of golds and reds and silvers. And became a crown of stars.

'None but the True One dares to wear the Crown of Stars. None but the True One can bear its weight and its heat. None but the True One can give the world back to the people and the magicks. When next the moon rises, I will fight for the world and take my crown. Will you follow me?'

They roared for her and cheered. The soldier and the farmer, the old and the young.

She sheathed her sword and passed her hand over the star so that its light slowly dimmed. 'Rest now,' she called out. 'Rest and gather your courage and your might. I go with my hawk, my wolf, and he who serves the dragon to prepare for the battle.'

When she would have leapt down, Thane circled her waist with his hands and lifted her to the ground. 'A queen shouldn't jump from a tree stump after so stirring a speech.'

'I need you to remind me of those small details.' Her lips curved at the smile in his eyes. 'And to look at me just like that, as often as possible.'

'I am at your service.'

'And now we need to gather our forces, and our brains. Gwayne? A quiet place where we four can speak?'

'May I serve here, my lady?' Kern asked, and at her nod, he flicked both wrists.

They stood now in a brightly lit chamber with a fire snapping in the hearth. Kern gestured toward a table and the chairs that surrounded it, 'This is my rath, and a good private place for plots and plans. Be comfortable. Would you have wine?'

'By the gods, I would,' Gwayne said, with feeling. 'It's been a dry march.'

'And food?' Platters of meat, bread, cheese, and fruit appeared on the table.

'No warrior eats until all eat,' Aurora said and earned a proud look from Gwayne.

'Your men will be fed, Majesty. We are pleased to offer our hospitality tonight.'

'Then eat.' She slapped Gwayne on the back. 'While I tell you what I know.'

She told him of the masque, of the dungeons, of the

threat to Brynn and Dira, and with Thane's help she drew diagrams of the fortifications and the locations of guards.

'Your father was a good friend,' Gwayne said to Thane, 'a brave warrior with a true heart. He would be proud to know what you have done, and will do.'

'Most of my life I've felt he would be ashamed I hadn't lifted my hand.'

'He loved your mother and you above all things. You have each sacrificed self for the life of the other. A man would be proud of such a wife, and such a son.'

'I don't want those sacrifices to be in vain,' Aurora added. 'Brynn and Dira must be protected, and Leia kept safe until the castle and city are back in our hands. Brynn and Dira's presence will be required at the masque. I want at least one man each by their side, to shield them, then to escort them to safety with Rhiann and Cyra.'

'There's an anteroom here.' Thane pointed to the drawings. 'With a passage gained by opening this panel by a mechanism in the hearth. My mother knows of it. Either she or Dira could lead the way from there.'

'It must be done quickly, before Lorcan thinks to use them as a bargaining tool. Just as freeing those in the dungeons must be done quickly. And quietly. We strike there first, while the company is gathered in the great hall for the masque. When it's done, we divide our troops. Into the tunnels to strike at the castle from the inside, to the walls – here and here?' She glanced at Thane for approval.

'The weakest points,' he agreed. 'A breach could be made, and from those three attacks, confining Lorcan and his personal guard between.'

She rose as Gwayne and Thane debated battle strategy, and she moved to the fire to study the images she saw in the flames.

She could hear the beat of her own heart, and knew it beat for revenge. There was a lust in her belly for blood – Lorcan's blood.

When she looked down at her hands, they were wet with it, and in her head were the agonized screams of the dying as her sword cut viciously through flesh and bone.

And in the flames she saw the Crown of Stars go black.

'Blood and death,' she declared when she sensed Kern behind her. 'If I hunger for this, what manner of queen am I?'

'Having hunger and sating appetite are different matters, lady.'

'I want this, for myself. His blood on my hands.' She held them up, knowing Kern could see as she saw. 'But it isn't for the good of the world, is it? To seek to take a life, even such a life as his, this is not light. It is not why I was made. Not why I am here.'

'To see that is power, and truth.'

'And still, I know there will be blood, there will be death. Of those I love, of those who follow me. I send them into battle and to the grave. This is the weight of power. Tonight, I turned my back on a young girl, knowing she would be ill used. Because if I had intervened, I might have betrayed the greater cause. But is there a greater cause, Kern, than the fate of a single innocent?'

'I don't rule. Such questions are part of a crown.'

'Yes, they are. I could do nothing else then. But now . . . It can be done another way. Am I strong enough to trust the crown instead of the sword? I've tested so little of my power to put such matters to it. To call the wind, a flock of birds . . . ' She wrapped her arms around herself. 'That's a game, not battle.'

'And you know what your sword can do.'

'Yes. I spoke the truth. I don't fear death in battle, but I fear the lives that will be lost on my account. And I fear what will become of me, and the world, if I take one if there's a choice. Thane trusts you. So will I.' She closed her eyes. 'Do you know what is in my mind?'

'I do, my lady.'

'And you'll help me.'

'I will.'

'Then we will plan for battle this way.' She glanced back at her teacher, and her lover. 'And hope for victory in another.'

10

The castle, the city, the countryside made ready for the masque. The prettiest maids were gathered up and brought in to serve and to decorate – and, Aurora noted, to serve *as* decoration. Farmers were ordered to offer their finest crops or livestock to the king in tribute. Wine and ale were hauled in on wagons, and without payment, so that the king and his guests could revel.

Portents were spoken of only in whispers. Lights, such great lights, seen in the forest at midnight. The stars that had circled into a crown in the night sky.

Open talk of such matters could lose a man his tongue.

Lords and ladies from all reaches of Twylia traveled to the City of Stars for the celebrations rather than displease the king who held them under his merciless thumb. Some with eligible daughters sent them to the hills or into caves, or into the Valley of Secrets, risking death or poverty. Others brought the maidens and prayed that the prince would pass their daughters over for others.

There were whispers, too, of rebellion, but the king ignored such foolishness and basked in the glory of the feast to come.

The dark glass showed no man who would claim his crown. And when he drank the blood of a sorcerer to bring visions, he saw only the shape of a wolf and the delicate hand of a woman who held the world in her palm.

He ordered his best hunters into the woods and the hills to track and kill any wolf. And garbed himself in his richest robes.

Time was short, and the risk worth taking. Armed, Thane hurried through the tunnels and chanced the daylight to find Gwayne.

'This isn't your place, or your time,' Gwayne told him. 'We are moving at sunset and still have much to prepare.'

'Lorcan sent six hunters out nearly an hour ago. They'll come this way. If they find you and even one escapes, you'll fight your battle here rather than on your chosen ground.'

'Are these men loyal to Lorcan?'

'Loyalty is cheap here.'

Gwayne fingered the hilt of his sword. 'Then we'd best offer them a dearer coin.'

Aurora chose white, the color of truth, for her gown. In her vision she had worn red, the color of blood. So she made this change deliberately, and hopefully. But not foolishly. The long, flowing sleeves hid the dagger she strapped to her wrist. Over Cyra's objections, she left her hair down, falling straight to her waist and unadorned. And in a gesture of pride and defiance, she pinned her mother's brooch to the gown between her breasts.

'He might recognize it,' Rhiann objected.

'If he does, it will be too late.' She took the globe and the star. 'I'll need these,' she slipped them into a white velvet purse. Turning from the looking glass, she held out her hands, one to Cyra, one to Rhiann. 'You've been mother and sister to me. Whatever changes tonight, nothing changes that. I ask that you see my beloved's mother and sister safe. If the light doesn't shine for the midnight hour, you're to take them to the Valley of Secrets, where Leia bides, and seek sanctuary. Your vow on it.'

'Aurora,' Rhiann began.

'Your vow on it,' Aurora insisted. 'I can only do what I must do with a clear heart and mind.'

'Then you have it. But the light will shine.'

Thane waited until the mounted hunter was directly below the bough, then leapt upon him. The force sent them both tumbling to the ground, and the alarmed horse shied.

Before a breath could be taken, Thane had his sword at the man's throat. 'Call out,' he said quietly, 'and it will be the last sound you make.'

'Thane of the stables?' There was as much shock as fear in the tone; 'What recklessness is this? I am on king's business.'

'It is a new day,' Thane said, then hauled the man to his feet. 'Take him off with the others.' He shoved the hunter toward two of the rebels who waited in the shelter of the trees. 'His bow and quiver will be useful. Tell Gwayne I've gone back. I will be listening.'

With a sense of purpose in every stride, he hurried back to the stables. Whatever happened, he would not pass another night there, sleeping on the floor like an animal.

Tonight his family would be free, and he would live – or die – in the service of his lady.

'You're late,' Kern complained the moment Thane climbed through the passage.

'I had business.'

'You've had considerable here as well, which I've seen to. Guests are still arriving, and their horses require care. You might have been missed if I hadn't been here to deal with it.'

'I'll tend the horses, then I am done with this. I swear if I have any say over what's done, whoever takes my place here will have decent quarters and payment for his labors.'

With some reluctance Thane unstrapped his sheath.

'I said I tended the horses. You've no need to labor over them again.' Lips pursed, Kern circled Thane. 'It will be considerable labor to tend to you.'

'What? What's wrong with me?'

Kern pinched one of Thane's ragged sleeves between his fingers. 'Nothing a bath and a barber and a tailor of some skill can't fix. But we've no time for all of that. I'll just have to see to it myself.'

'I don't need a bloody barber before a battle.'

'You need one before a masque. But the bath first. Believe me, you can use one.'

295

Kern snapped his fingers twice and conjured a copper tub full of steaming water.

'I'm not going to the masque, but to the dungeons to help free the prisoners. I don't think they'll care if I smell sweet or not.'

'The prisoners are being freed even now.'

'Now?' Even as Thane reached for his sword, Kern waved a hand. And Thane was naked.

'For the sake of the gods!'

'You're not needed. My kind are adept at getting into locked places.' Kern grinned. 'We enjoy it. You'll be needed at the masque, and you won't get past the guards unless you're bathed, groomed, and properly attired. The tub, boy.'

'I'll stand with Gwayne, lead—' He found himself in the tub, immersed. He came up sputtering.

'You waste breath arguing. Are you afraid to go to a ball?'

'I'm not going to dance, thundering hell. I'm going to fight.'

'And so you may. But if and when, you fight by her side. To get to her side, you need what I'll give you. Wash.' Kern circled the tub while Thane sulked and scrubbed.

'Is this the queen's bidding?'

'No. But she will be pleased enough. It is her wish and her will to take the throne with as little blood as possible.

The magicks have agreed to aid her in this,' he added as Thane's head came up sharply. 'We will enchant the guards to sleep, and the walls will be breached without sword. No man will die in the city or outside the keep. But inside, Lorcan's power must be faced and vanquished, or she cannot rule. There is the battle. Dark against light. The pure against the corrupt. And there you must be.'

Kern tapped his finger to his lips, considering as Thane hauled himself out of the tub. 'Simplicity, I think,' he stated and, wagging his finger, garbed Thane in royal blue with tiny flecks of gold. 'No, no, not quite.'

Thane scowled at the lace spilling over his wrists. 'I feel like a fool.'

'As long as you don't behave as one, we'll have no problem.' He changed the blue to black, the gold to silver, and nodding, drew Thane's hair back in a short queue. 'Dress swords only.' He snapped and had a jeweled-handled sword in the silver sheath.

Pleased for the first time by the turn of events, Thane drew the sword. 'A fine weapon. Good balance.'

'It was your father's.'

Thane lowered the sword and stared into the eyes of his teacher. 'Thank you. I fail, too often, to thank you.'

'Meet your destiny, and that is thanks enough. One last

touch.' Kern waved a hand and covered the top of Thane's face with a black domino.

'Take your place,' Kern said quietly. 'Stay true to your blood and your heart. The world rests on what passes tonight.'

Aurora held herself straight, fixed a flirtatious smile on her face, and stepped into the great hall. Music was playing, and already lines were set for dancing. Tables groaned with platters of food, and hundreds of candles streamed light.

Dress was elaborate, with feathers and furs, high head-dresses and flowing trains. She saw Lorcan drinking deeply of wine, with his queen pale and silent beside him.

The first order, she thought, was to separate them so Brynn and Dira could be spirited away to safety. Despite the masks and costumes, she had little trouble in locating Owen and staying out of his line of sight. She walked directly to the king, curtsied.

'Majesty, my humble thanks for the invitation to so lively a celebration.'

'The voice is familiar, as is ... the form.' He tapped a finger under his chin, studied her smile and the eyes that looked out of a sparkling silver mask. 'What is the name?'

'Sire, the guessing is the game.' She trailed a finger down

his arm in a daring move. 'At least until the hour strikes twelve and we are unmasked. Might I beg for a cup of wine?'

'Asking is enough.' He snapped his fingers and a servant hurryied over. Deliberately, Aurora shifted to look back at the dancing, and had Lorcan turning his back on his wife. 'Would you care to take a turn of the room with me?'

'Delighted and charmed.' He offered her his arm. 'I believe I have guessed this game, Lady Aurora. You are, I believe, the most daring of the maidens here.'

'One expects a king to be wise and clever, and you are, sire.' She lifted her glass as they walked, and saw Rhiann nod. The first move would be made.

She chattered, commenting on the costumes, complimenting the music, knowing that she would soon circle toward Owen. But while she did, Brynn and Dira would be safely away. As would her own women.

'Lovely lady.' Aurora's heart stopped at the voice when the courtier in black bowed in front of her. 'Might I steal you away for a dance?'

Struggling to gather her scattered wits, she inclined her head. 'If His Majesty permits.'

'Yes, yes, go.' He waved her away and held out his cup for more wine.

'Are you mad?' Aurora said under her breath.

'If love is madness, I am so afflicted.' Thane led her across the room, and hoped it was far enough away. 'But the fact is, I don't dance. Would that I did. You are so beautiful tonight.'

'Do something,' she hissed.

'I'll feed you.' He began to pile a plate with delicacies. 'It's something flirtatious courtiers do for ladies at balls – so I've seen when I've spied on them. Sugarplum?' Grinning, he held one up to her lips.

She bit in and laughed. 'You are mad. I'm so glad to see you. I want to touch you, and dare not. Your mother and sister are being taken to safety.'

'I saw them go. I can never repay you.'

'Learn to dance, then one day promise to dance with me.'

'On my oath. If I could, I would whisk you out on the terrace, kiss your lips in the light of the rising moon. And there would only be music and moonlight for us.' He took her hand, brushed a kiss over it. 'I know what you've planned with the magicks. You should have told me.'

'I was afraid you and Gwayne would never agree. You wish for blood – both of you, and you've earned it – both of you. I'm denying you your right.'

'I would not have agreed.' His eyes lifted to hers with a

sudden shock of power. 'I do not agree. There are bruises on your throat, beloved. You didn't quite cover them.'

'Have they any more import than those he put on you?'

'Yes. Oh, yes.'

'Find another kitten to stroke.' Owen snapped out the order, shoving Thane aside. Even as Thane's hand gripped the hilt of his sword, Aurora stepped between them. 'Sir,' she said lightly to Owen, 'I am no kitten.'

'A cat, more like, rubbing herself against any willing leg.'

'If you think so of me, I'm surprised you would spend a moment in my company.' She started to turn away, resisted when Owen took her arm. With her back to him she mouthed *Not yet* to Thane, then faced Owen once more. 'You make a spectacle of us, my lord. The king will not approve.'

Owen took her hand, squeezing until her fingers ground bone to bone. He leaned close and spoke in a voice like silk. 'I will not choose you. But I will have you. Had you been more agreeable, you would have been queen.'

She saw two of the king's personal guards rush into the hall, heard the clamor, and knew the rebels were over the walls and through the tunnels.

She stepped back and, over the shouts, spoke clearly. 'I am queen.'

11

'You will have nothing,' she said. 'For nothing is what you have earned. Your time is ended, and mine begins. The hour is about to strike.'

'No woman speaks so to me.' Owen drew back his hand. And Thane's sword was out and at his throat.

'Touch her, and I will slice your hand off at the wrist.' With his free hand Thane pulled off his mask. 'Don't interfere,' he said to Aurora. 'I'm not a man if I don't stand for myself and my lady, at long last.'

'Your lady,' Owen spat.

'My lady, and my queen.' Thane stepped back a pace. 'Draw your sword.'

Chaos was already reigning as guards battled the rebels who charged into the hall. Lords and courtiers dragged screaming women away from the fray, or simply left them and scrambled for cover themselves. Aurora cast aside her own mask and called out for a sword. She would have no choice now but to fight her way to Lorcan and cut off any chance of escape.

Owen pulled his sword. 'Stableboy, I will cut you apart, piece by piece, and feed you to my dogs.'

With a thin smile, Thane made a mocking salute with his sword. 'Will you fight, you tedious braggart, or simply talk me to death?'

Owen came in fast, striking, thrusting, and Thane felt his blood sing. Their swords crossed, slid hilt to hilt, and he grinned between the lethal vee. 'I have dreamed of this.'

'You dream your own death.'

They broke apart, and steel flashed against steel.

Wielding a sword of her own, Aurora slashed blades aside, shoved a swooning woman into a courtier's arms, then whirled to fight back to back with Gwayne.

'Outside?' she shouted. 'The walls, the tunnels.'

'It's done. This is all that's left. The faeries hold them fast, and the dungeons are clear.'

'Then we end this.' She looked toward Lorcan and saw his sword was bright with blood. 'We take him.'

With Gwayne, she fought her way to the king. They battled through the panicked guests, leaping over the fallen and the fainting to be joined by others as she called them to arms. They pressed the outnumbered guards to the walls, and Aurora locked swords with Lorcan.

'You may take me,' she said calmly. 'I think you won't, but you may. If you do, these men will cut you down. You will not live through this night unless you lay down your sword.'

'You will be hanged.' His eyes burned black. There was blood on his hands, she saw. As there was on hers. 'You will be drawn, quartered, and hanged.'

'Lay down your sword, Lorcan the usurper, or I will end this in death after all.'

'There will be death.' But he threw down his sword. 'It will be yours.'

'Tell your guards to lay down their weapons. You're outnumbered here. Tell them to lay down their weapons so you might hear my terms.'

'Enough!' He shouted it with Aurora's sword to his throat. 'Lay down your swords. Your king commands you.'

The sounds of clashing steel dimmed until there was only Thane's blade against Owen's.

'Let him finish,' she said to Gwayne. 'The hour has not yet struck. This is his time, not mine, and he must live it. Put Lorcan on the throne he values so much, and hold him there.'

Across the hall the two men fought like demons. Winded, Owen hacked and cleaved, and cursed when Thane's sword flicked his away. Enraged, he grabbed a candlestand and heaved it, following with vicious sweeps as Thane dodged aside and spun back into attack.

'You are too used to sparring with soldiers who are beaten or banished if they dare best you,' Thane taunted. 'Now that it's your life—' Thane slashed, and cut neatly through Owen's silk doublet to score the flesh – 'You're clumsy.'

'You are *nothing*! Coward, whipping boy.'

'I carry your scars.' Thane sliced the point of his sword down Owen's cheek. 'Now you carry mine. And that is enough.'

With two quick thrusts, he knocked Owen's sword out of his hand, then pressed his own to his enemy's belly. 'I won't kill you, as I wish you many years of life. Years of misery and humiliation. On your knees before your Majesty.'

'I will not kneel to you.'

'It is not to me you kneel. But to her.' He stepped aside, shifting his sword point to the back of Owen's neck so the man could see Aurora standing among the fallen and the frightened.

'You are,' she said to Thane, 'what I have always wished for. What I will always prize. In the midst of battle, when vengeance was your right, you chose honor.'

'Whore!' Owen shrieked it. 'Drab. She lay on her back for me. She—'

Thane shifted his grip on the sword and slammed the hilt into the side of Owen's head. When Owen fell unconscious, Thane booted him carelessly aside. 'I'm not perfect,' he said with a flashing smile, and Aurora laughed.

'I believe you may be. The hour comes.' She could feel the power rising in her. 'I almost wish it wouldn't. That we could walk away, and live in a cottage in the woods or ramble across the world in a wagon. I almost wish it, but it comes and I have no choice.'

'A cottage, a world, a crown. It's all the same to me, if I'm with you.'

'Stand with me, then.' She turned and faced Lorcan as he sprawled on the throne under the swords of her men. 'Lower your swords, step back. Open the doors, the windows. Let the people in, let them know what happens here at the witching hour, at my hour. Lorcan, stand and face me as you did not face my father or my mother. I am Aurora. I am the Lady of the Light. I am the True One.'

She walked toward him as she spoke and flung out her arms. 'Are there any here in this company, any here in the City of Stars, in the world, who will not pledge their loyalty to the True One? For they are free to leave this place, and to go in peace. There will not be blood or death.'

'You're nothing but a woman, a whore, as my son has said. I am king. The True One is a myth babbled by madmen.'

'Behold the dragon!' She pointed toward the window, and the fire that lit the sky in the shape of a dragon.

'A witch's trick.' He rose and, pushing out with his hand, shot a fierce wind through the hall. It blew her hair back, set her gown to billowing. The sharpness of it sliced her hand and drew blood. But she stood against it.

'You would match your power to mine?' She arched her brows. 'Here is the world, stained by my blood, and the blood of my people.' She drew the crystal globe from her purse, threw it high so it spun near the ceiling and showered light and spilled out voices raised in song. 'Take it if you dare. And here is the crown, the Crown of Stars.'

She reached in her purse again and flung the star. It flew in dizzying circles and exploded with light.

She stood, draped in billowing white, unarmed, and waited while the bells began to strike midnight. 'And this is my hour, the hour of my birth and beginnings. The hour of life and death, of power and portent. The time between time when day meets day and night meets night.'

The crown circled, beamed light, and descended toward her head.

Lifting her arms, she accepted her destiny. 'And in this hour, the reign of dark is ended and the reign of light begins. I am the True One, and this is my world to protect.'

The crown settled on her head, and every man and woman, every soldier and servant, fell to their knees.

Outside, the people who massed could be heard chanting her name like a prayer.

'I am Aurora, descendant of Draco, daughter of Gwynn and Rhys. I am queen of Twylia.'

On a roar, Lorcan grabbed the sword from a dazzled rebel and, raising it high, lunged toward Aurora. Murder was in his cry, madness was in his eyes.

And springing like a wolf, Thane leapt forward, spinning to shield her, and ran Lorcan through.

He fell at her feet with his blood splashing the white hem

of her gown. With the stars still gleaming on her head, she looked down on him with a pity that was cold as winter.

'So . . . So it ends in death after all. He made his choice. The debt is paid. My father and yours.' She turned to Thane, held out her hand. 'My mother and yours.'

The last bell struck, and the wind died. Her crown sparkled like stars.

'What was taken in blood is restored. In blood. Now let there be peace. Open the larders,' she ordered. 'Feed the people of the city. No one goes hungry tonight.'

'My lady.' Gwayne knelt before her. 'The people call for you. They call for their queen. Will you go out so they can see you?'

'I will. Only a moment first. A moment,' she repeated and turned to Thane. 'It will be hard. After the joy, it will be hard. There will be work and sweat and time to restore faith, to bring order, to renew trust. There will be so much to do. I need you beside me.'

'I am the queen's man, my lady.' He brought her hand to his lips. Then with a laugh born of freedom, he lifted her off her feet, and high above his head. 'Beloved. Woman of my visions, mother of my son. My light. My life.'

She wrapped her arms around him, tipped her mouth to his for the warmth and power of his kiss as he spun her in circles. 'Then there's nothing I can't do. Nothing we can't be.'

'We'll be happy.'

'Yes. Till the end of days.'

With her hand linked with his, she walked out to the cheers of the people of the world.

And they raised her up to be queen, Aurora, the Light.

IF YOU ENJOYED THESE STORIES
KEEP READING FOR A SPECIAL PREVIEW
OF

THE WITNESS

AVAILABLE NOW FROM PIATKUS

June 2000

Elizabeth Fitch's short-lived teenage rebellion began with L'Oréal Pure Black, a pair of scissors and a fake ID. It ended in blood.

For nearly the whole of her sixteen years, eight months and twenty-one days she'd dutifully followed her mother's directives. Dr. Susan L. Fitch issued *directives,* not orders. Elizabeth had adhered to the schedules her mother created, ate the meals designed by her mother's nutritionist and prepared by her mother's cook, wore the clothes selected by her mother's personal shopper.

Dr. Susan L. Fitch dressed conservatively, as suited—in her opinion— her position as chief of surgery of Chicago's Silva Memorial Hospital. She expected, and directed, her daughter to do the same.

Elizabeth studied diligently, accepting and excelling in the academic programs her mother outlined. In the fall, she'd return to Harvard in pursuit of her medical degree. So she could become a doctor, like her mother—a surgeon, like her mother.

Elizabeth—never Liz or Lizzie or Beth—spoke fluent Spanish, French, Italian, passable Russian and rudimentary Japanese. She played both piano and violin. She'd traveled to Europe, to Africa. She could name all the bones, nerves and muscles in the human body and play Chopin's Piano Concerto—both Nos. 1 and 2, by rote.

She'd never been on a date or kissed a boy. She'd never roamed the mall with a pack of girls, attended a slumber party or giggled with friends over pizza or hot fudge sundaes.

She was, at sixteen years, eight months and twenty-one days, a product of her mother's meticulous and detailed agenda.

That was about to change.

She watched her mother pack. Susan, her rich brown hair already coiled in her signature French twist, neatly hung another suit in the organized garment bag, then checked off the printout with each day of the week's medical conference broken into subgroups. The printout included a spreadsheet listing every event, appointment, meeting and meal, sched-uled with the selected outfit, with shoes, bag and accessories.

Designer suits; Italian shoes, of course, Elizabeth thought.

One must wear good cuts, good cloth. But not one rich or bright color among the blacks, grays, taupes. She wondered how her mother could be so beautiful and deliberately wear the dull.

After two accelerated semesters of college, Elizabeth thought she'd begun—maybe—to develop her own fashion sense. She had, in fact, bought jeans *and* a hoodie *and* some chunky-heeled boots in Cambridge.

With cash, so the receipt wouldn't show up on her credit card bill, in case her mother or their accountant checked and questioned the items, which were currently hidden in her room.

She'd felt like a different person wearing them, so different she'd walked straight into a McDonald's and ordered her first Big Mac with large fries and a chocolate shake.

The pleasure had been so huge, she'd had to go into the bathroom, close herself in a stall and cry a little.

The seeds of the rebellion had been planted that day, she supposed, or maybe they'd always been there, dormant, and the fat and salt had awakened them.

But she could feel them, actually feel them, sprouting in her belly now.

"Your plans changed, Mother. It doesn't follow that mine have to change with them."

Susan took a moment to precisely place a shoe bag in the Pullman, tucking it just so with her beautiful and clever surgeon's hands, the nails perfectly manicured. A French manicure, as always—no color there, either.

"Elizabeth." Her voice was as polished and calm as her wardrobe. "It took considerable effort to reschedule and have you admitted to the summer program this term. You'll complete the requirements for your admission into Harvard Medical School a full semester ahead of schedule."

Even the thought made Elizabeth's stomach hurt. "I was promised a three-week break, including this next week in New York."

"And sometimes promises must be broken. If I hadn't had this coming week off, I couldn't fill in for Dr. Dusecki at the conference."

"You could have said no."

"That would have been selfish and shortsighted." Susan brushed at the jacket she'd hung, stepped back to check her list. "You're certainly mature enough to understand the demands of work overtake pleasure and leisure."

"If I'm mature enough to understand that, why aren't I mature enough to make my own decisions? I want this break. I need it."

Susan barely spared her daughter a glance. "A girl of your

age, physical condition and mental acumen hardly *needs* a break from her studies and activities. In addition, Mrs. Laine has already left for her two-week cruise, and I could hardly ask her to postpone her vacation. There's no one to fix your meals or tend to the house."

"I can fix my own meals and tend the house."

"Elizabeth." The tone managed to merge clipped with long-suffering. It's settled."

"And I have no say in it? What about developing my independence, being responsible?"

"Independence comes in degrees, as does responsibility and freedom choice. You still require guidance and direction. Now, I've e-mailed you an updated schedule for the coming week, and your packet with the information on the program is on your desk. Be sure to thank Dr. Frisco personally for making room for you in the summer term."

As she spoke, Susan closed the garment bag, then her small Pullman. He stepped to her bureau to check her hair, her lipstick.

"You don't listen to anything I say."

In the mirror, Susan's gaze shifted to her daughter. The first time, Elizabeth thought, her mother had bothered to actually look at her since she'd come into the bedroom. "Of course I do. I heard everything you said, very clearly."

"Listening's different than hearing."

"That may be true, Elizabeth, but we've already had this discussion."

"It's not a discussion, it's a decree."

Susan's mouth tightened briefly, the only sign of annoyance. When she turned, her eyes were coolly, calmly blue. "I'm sorry you feel that way. As your mother, I must do what I believe best for you."

"What's best for me, in your opinion, is for me to do, be, say, think, act, want, become exactly what you decided for me before you inseminated yourself with precisely selected sperm."

She heard the rise of her own voice but couldn't control it, felt the hot sting of tears in her eyes but couldn't stop them. "I'm tired of being your experiment. I'm tired of having every minute of every day organized, orchestrated and choreographed to meet your expectations. I want to make my own choices, buy my own clothes, read books *I* want to read. I want to live my own life instead of yours."

Susan's eyebrows lifted in an expression of mild interest. "Well. Your attitude isn't surprising, given your age, but you've picked a very inconvenient time to be defiant and argumentative."

"Sorry. It wasn't on the schedule."

"Sarcasm's also typical, but it's unbecoming." Susan opened her briefcase, checked the contents. "We'll talk about all this when I get back. I'll make an appointment with Dr. Bristoe."

"I don't need therapy! I need a mother who *listens*, who gives a shit about how I feel."

"That kind of language only shows a lack of maturity and intellect."

Enraged, Elizabeth threw up her hands, spun in circles. If she couldn't be calm and rational like her mother, she'd be *wild*. "Shit! Shit! Shit!"

"And repetition hardly enhances. You have the rest of the weekend to consider your behavior. Your meals are in the refrigerator or freezer, and labeled. Your pack list is on your desk. Report to Ms. Vee at the university at eight on Monday morning. Your participation in this program will ensure your place in HMS next fall. Now, take my garment bag downstairs, please. My car will be here any minute."

Oh, those seeds were sprouting, cracking that fallow ground and pushing painfully through. For the first time in her life, Elizabeth looked straight into her mother's eyes and said, "No."

She spun around, stomped away and slammed the door

of her bedroom. She threw herself down on the bed, stared at the ceiling with tear-blurred eyes. And waited.

Any second, any second, she told herself. Her mother would come in, demand an apology, demand obedience. And Elizabeth wouldn't give one, either.

They'd have a fight, an actual fight, with threats of punishment and consequences. Maybe they'd yell at each other. Maybe if they yelled, her mother would finally hear her.

And maybe, if they yelled, she could say all the things that had crept up inside her this past year. Things she thought now had been inside her forever.

She didn't want to be a doctor. She didn't want to spend every waking hour on a schedule or hide a stupid pair of jeans because they didn't fit her mother's dress code.

She wanted to have friends, not approved socialization appointments. She wanted to listen to the music girls her age listened to. She wanted to know what they whispered about and laughed about and talked about while she was shut out.

She didn't want to be a genius or a prodigy.

She wanted to be normal. She just wanted to be like everyone else.

She swiped at the tears, curled up, stared at the door.

Any second, she thought again. Any second now. Her

mother had to be angry. She had to come in and assert authority. Had to.

"Please," Elizabeth murmured as seconds ticked into minutes. "Don't make me give in again. Please, please, don't make me give up."

Love me enough. Just this once.

But as the minutes dragged on, Elizabeth pushed herself off the bed. Patience, she knew, was her mother's greatest weapon. That, and the unyielding sense of being right, crushed all foes. And certainly her daughter was no match for it.

Defeated, she walked out of her room, toward her mother's.

The garment bag, the briefcase, the small, wheeled Pullman were gone. Even as she walked downstairs, she knew her mother had gone, too.

"She left me. She just left."

Alone, she looked around the pretty, tidy living room. Everything perfect—the fabrics, the colors, the art, the arrangement. The antiques passed down through generations of Fitches—all quiet elegance.

Empty.

Nothing had changed, she realized. And nothing would.

"So I will."

She didn't allow herself to think, to question or second-guess. Instead, she marched back up, snagged scissors from her study area.

In her bathroom, she studied her face in the mirror—coloring she'd gotten through paternity—auburn hair, thick like her mother's but without the soft, pretty wave. Her mother's high, sharp cheekbones, her biological father's—whoever he was—deep-set green eyes, pale skin, wide mouth.

Physically attractive, she thought, because that was DNA and her mother would tolerate no less. But not beautiful, not striking like Susan, no. And that, she supposed, had been a disappointment even her mother couldn't fix.

"Freak." Elizabeth pressed a hand to the mirror, hating what she saw in the glass. "You're a freak. But as of now, you're not a coward."

Taking a big breath, she yanked up a hunk of her shoulder-length hair and whacked it off.

With every snap of the scissors she felt empowered. *Her* hair, *her* choice. She let the shorn hanks fall on the floor. As she snipped and hacked, an image formed in her mind. Eyes narrowed, head angled, she slowed the clipping. It was just geometry, really, she decided—and physics. Action and reaction.

The weight—physical and metaphorical, she thought—

just fell away. And the girl in the glass looked lighter. Her eyes seemed bigger, her face not so thin, not so drawn.

She looked . . . new, Elizabeth decided.

Carefully, she set the scissors down, and, realizing her breath was heaving in and out, made a conscious effort to slow it.

So short. Testing, she lifted a hand to her exposed neck, ears, then brushed them over the bangs she'd cut. Too even, she decided. She hunted up manicure scissors, tried her hand at styling.

Not bad. Not really good, she admitted, but different. That was the whole point. She looked, and felt, different.

But not finished.

Leaving the hair where it lay on the floor, she went into her bedroom, changed into her secret cache of clothes. She needed product—that's what the girls called it. Hair product. And makeup. And more clothes.

She needed the mall.

Riding on the thrill, she went into her mother's home office, took the spare car keys. And her heart hammered with excitement as she hurried to the garage. She got behind the wheel, shut her eyes a moment. "Here we go," she said quietly, then hit the garage-door opener and backed out.

She got her ears pierced. It seemed a bold if mildly painful move, and suited the hair dye she'd taken from the shelf after a long, careful study and debate. She bought hair wax, as she'd seen one of the girls at college use it and thought she could duplicate the look. More or less.

She bought two hundred dollars' worth of makeup because she wasn't sure what was right.

Then she had to sit down because her knees shook. But she wasn't done, Elizabeth reminded herself, as she watched the packs of teenagers, groups of women, teams of families, wander by. She just needed to regroup.

She needed clothes, but she didn't have a plan, a list, an agenda. Impulse buying was exhilarating, and exhausting. The temper that had driven her this far left her with a dull headache, and her earlobes throbbed a little.

The logical, sensible thing to do was go home, lie down for a while. Then plan, make that list of items to be purchased.

But that was the old Elizabeth. This one was just going to catch her breath.

The problem facing her now was that she wasn't precisely sure which store or stores she should go to. There were so many of them, and all the windows full of *things*. So she'd wander, watch for girls her age. She'd go where they went.

She gathered her bags, pushed to her feet—and bumped into someone.

"Excuse me," she began, then recognized the girl. "Oh. Julie."

"Yeah." The blonde with the sleek, perfect hair and melted-chocolate eyes gave Elizabeth a puzzled look. "Do I know you?"

"Probably not. We went to school together. I was student teacher in your Spanish class. Elizabeth Fitch."

"Elizabeth, sure. The brain trust." Julie narrowed her sulky eyes. "You look different."

"Oh. I . . ." Embarrassed now, Elizabeth lifted a hand to her hair. "I cut my hair."

"Cool. I thought you moved away or something."

"I went to college. I'm home for the summer."

"Oh, yeah, you graduated early. Weird."

"I suppose it is. Will you go to college this fall?"

"I'm supposed to go to Brown."

"That's a wonderful school."

"Okay. Well . . ."

"Are you shopping?"

"Broke." Julie shrugged—and Elizabeth took a survey of her outfit—the snug jeans, riding very low on the hipbones, the skinny, midriff-baring shirt, the oversized shoulder bag and wedge sandals. "I just came to the mall to see my boyfriend—my *ex*-boyfriend, since I broke up with him."

"I'm sorry."

"Screw him. He works at the Gap. We were supposed to go out tonight, and now he says he has to work till ten, then wants to hang out with his bros after. I've had it, so I dumped him."

Elizabeth started to point out that he shouldn't be penalized for honoring his obligations, but Julie kept talking—and it occurred to Elizabeth that the other girl hadn't spoken more than a dozen words to her since they'd known each other.

"So I'm going over to Tiffany's, see if she wants to hang, because now I've got no boyfriend for the summer. It sucks. I guess you hang out with college guys." Julie gave her a considering look. "Go to frat parties, keggers, all that."

"I . . . There are a lot of men at Harvard."

"Harvard." Julie rolled her eyes. "Any of them in Chicago for the summer?"

"I couldn't say."

"A college guy, that's what I need. Who wants some loser who works at the mall? I need somebody who knows how to have fun, who can take me places, buy alcohol. Good luck with that, unless you can get into the clubs. That's where they hang out. Just need to score some fake ID."

"I can do that." The instant the words were out, Elizabeth wondered where they'd come from. But Julie gripped her arm, smiled at her as if they were friends.

"No bull?"

"No. That is, it's not very difficult to create false identification with the right tools. A template, photo, laminate, a computer with Photo-shop."

"Brain trust. What'll it take for you to make me a driver's license that'll get me into a club?"

"As I said, a template—"

"No, Jesus. What do you want for it?"

"I . . ." Bargaining, Elizabeth realized. A barter. "I need to buy some clothes, but I don't know what I should buy. I need someone to help me."

"A shopping buddy?"

"Yes. Someone who knows. You know."

Eyes no longer sulky, voice no longer bored, Julie simply beamed. "That's *my* brain trust. And if I help you pick out some outfits, you'll make me up the ID?"

"Yes. And I'd also want to go with you to the club. So I'd need the right clothes for that, too."

"You? Clubbing? More than your hair's changed, Liz."

Liz. She was Liz. "I'd need a photo, and it will take a little while to construct the IDs. I could have them done tomorrow. What club would we go to?"

"Might as well go for the hottest club in town. Warehouse 12. Brad Pitt went there when he was in town."

"Do you know him?"

"I wish. Okay, let's go shopping."

It made her dizzy, not just the way Julie piloted her into a store, snatched up clothes with only the most cursory study. But the *idea* of it all. A shopping buddy. Not someone who preselected what was deemed appropriate and expected her to assent. Someone who grabbed at random and talked about looking hot, or cool, even sexy.

No one had ever suggested to Elizabeth that she might look sexy.